PRASE F(

HORROR FROM THE HIGH DIVE
VOLUME 1

"*Horror From The High Dive* is incredibly fun with lots of scares, surprises, and sharp wit... I couldn't stop reading. I'd highly recommend diving into this very original and fantastic anthology!"

— Larry Postel, Award-winning WGA screenwriter of
The Main Event, Flip Turn, and High Holiday

"*Horror From The High Dive* is a creepy crawling good time! Reunited with all the monsters that scared us as kids, this compilation of frightful short stories is one you'll definitely want to sink your teeth into. It's perfect for spooky season — and all year long. Best read in the dark with a flashlight!"

— @TurnsMyPage, Book Blog

"Every horror anthology should have some hidden gems. *Horror from the High Dive* has more than its share."

— Del Howison, Stoker Award-winning editor for Dark Delicacies

"Spooky and funny — the perfect read for Halloween (or if you want to feel like it's Halloween any time of year). It reminded me of the scary story books I dared myself to get out of the library as a kid."

— Madeline Walter, Writer, Brooklyn Nine-Nine

"Awesome collection that ranges from fun and spooky to truly disturbing. Great work by some of my favorite indie authors. "

— Becca Spence Dobias, Author, On Home

Published by

 HIGH DIVE
PUBLISHING

www.HighDivePublishing.com

HighDivePublishing@gmail.com

Twitter @HighDivePublish

Instagram @HighDivePublishing

Cover illustration by Chris Copeland

Book design by Megan Katsanevakis

This collection of stories is dedicated to the young people (and any one else who hasn't quite grown up all the way yet) who **SEEK OUT SCARES**, find *FUN IN FRIGHTS*, and search for that forgotten shelf in the back of the library where the truly terrifying tales reside. We hope that each of you finds something *A LITTLE SPOOKY* in the following stories.

Horror From

The High Dive

VOLUME 1

ADAMS • BADEWITZ • CABELLO
CAMERON • DUNFORD • FORRISTER
GREENE • HARMON • HARTWELL
JOHNSON • LEE • MALONE • MEDINA

TABLE OF CONTENTS

Read On If You Dare

by K.C. Dunford

Withered leaves gusting
Ears teasing, dirt scraping
Trip through the door just in time
Slam shut, twist the deadbolt
Burn the wick of a candle
Just enough light to read by.

Finger bones aching
Teeth tapping, hands shaking
Goosebumps and hairs standing high
Crack open these stories
And you won't sleep a stitch
You belong to these pages tonight.

Welcome to the eerie
And ghostly, uncanny
Stories unsettling and strange
Go on if you dare
But readers beware
Some nightmares don't stay on the page.

Do Zombies Eat Mozzarella Sticks?

by Peter L. Harmon

I'm not sure exactly when they started staggering in. It was certainly within the time frame that I was in the guard office, counting the day's receipts, because as I headed back to the snack bar to lock up for the night, I saw Roheed, my assistant manager, a smart but shy young man with dark hair and brown eyes, hauling ass to the back door of the snack bar, garbage water still dripping from his hands.

Roheed had begun mopping and doing the dishes and collecting trash from the various receptacles as I had shoveled the wet bills and grimy dimes into the cash box to take over to the guard office to load into the safe. Roheed had put all of the refuse into an industrial-sized dark-green garbage bag and dragged it over to the dumpster, leaving a snail trail of old soda that had lost its carbonation, congealed nacho cheese flavored goo, and fry grease in its wake.

But as I returned to the snack bar at the Yellow County Community Swim and Racquet Club that early September day, as Autumn was just beginning to threaten its impending return, I heard Roheed screaming in a tone that I hadn't really heard from him before, something about "They're dead, they're all dead and they're coming to the pool!"

I wasn't sure what to make of Roheed's antics, but he looked scared as hell and I decided to run first, ask questions later. So we both booked it to the snack shack and bolted the door once we were inside.

Roheed was still jibbering and jabbering and I couldn't get a coherent sentence from him, so I decided to have a look-see for myself. That's when I saw one for the first time.

As I looked through the green metal grate that we pulled shut and locked at closing time, after the evening dinner rush, when families who had swum all day and now needed nourishment to make the drive back to DC or walk up the steep hill that led out of the racquet club back to town, I saw what I thought was just one of the older teens goofing off on the high dive. Even though the pool was about to close, sometimes the seniors from East Yellow High would roll into the swim club near twilight to do increasingly dangerous dives off the 10 meter board until Jonathan, the Head Lifeguard in Charge, kicked them out.

But this wasn't that.

I squinted at the goings on from the snack bar window to the pool deck down the hill, about a stone's throw away, if you could throw a stone hella far, probably more like an arrow's shot if you weren't great at shooting arrows, and who is these days?

It was sunset, magic hour, and there were pinks commingling with purples near the tree line of the tall trees that surrounded the pool compound. The sun was a fiery red dodgeball.

The figure on the high dive was walking erratically towards the end of the board in cutoffs (I learned later that they could more accurately be described as "ripped-offs" because the thing had ripped the pant legs off below its knee when they had gotten snagged on the chain link fence that surrounded the pool compound) and instead of taking a big bounce or two at the end of the board and launching itself into the water with a dive or any kind of flourish, the thing or being or whatever you want to call it, simply walked to the end of the board and tipped forward, legs still shuffling onward, as if it didn't know where the diving board ended and the evening air began.

"That was Mayor O'Houlihan," Roheed told me at that point. That sounded ridiculous to me. Mayor O'Houlihan had better things to do than take a dive into the 12-foot deep pool well on a Wednesday at dusk in the middle of campaign season. He was running for re-election for goodness sake (unopposed sure, but still).

I looked back at the pool and sure enough, Mayor O'Houlihan's head peeked out of the 6-foot then 5-foot deep section of the pool as he ambled forward. He was head and shoulders and chest out of the 4-foot when he came to the barrier that separated the main pool from the gentle incline of the kiddie beach area. The mushroom fountain was of course turned off for the evening.

And that's when I noticed that something was not right with Mayor O'Houlihan; he was just ambling aimlessly forward, bumping into the barrier over and over without changing his direction. He was still far from my perch, as I was peering out of the snack bar's *Order* window, but I could now make out some of his features. His eyes were lolled back into his head, his mouth agape. His skin seemed to be a barf-greenish color, but I wasn't sure if the waning light and the reflection from the blue of the pool floor or the ripple of the water was playing a trick on my eyes.

He was also missing an arm, simply a stump where that appendage used to be. Black veins spiraled outward from the wound and up into the mayor's neck. I don't know how I didn't catch that first thing.

"Looks like we're going to need to elect a new mayor," I

said more to myself than to Roheed.

Things were starting to add up as I saw more erect bodies lurching around the swim and racquet club compound, some with dark maroon blood caked around their gaping maws, some still chewing on the flesh of other former Yellow County residents. One with a pool towel draped around its shoulders, as if it had been overtaken by whatever hellish disease or affliction this was right as it had been drying off after a day's swim.

"Roheed," I said to Roheed, "you didn't tell me there were damned zombies out there."

He was still trying to make sense of it all himself, breathing heavily, sitting on a wooden stool near the three basin sink.

"I didn't want to say it out loud," he said, "for fear that it was true."

We were in a bigger pickle than one of the large kosher deli sized pickles we had in the refrigerator at the time, swimming in green brine ($1 each). We were trapped in the Yellow County Community Swim and Racquet Club snack bar, surrounded by brainless yet brain-craving zombies. At least I assumed they were brain-craving, due to the shenanigans that were taking place over on the clay tennis courts. Several of the creatures had ganged up on two tennis-playing seniors: a couple of Wheezers and Geezers (the unofficial name the older tennis playing folks had given themselves with a wink) that were trying to get a few thwacks in before the pool closed. The horde was taking big bites of flesh from the pair, bright red spurts that looked like ketchup glorping onto their tennis whites.

One zombie had the old man's head cracked open like a soft boiled egg and was eating his brain like it was participating in a Fourth of July cherry pie eating contest.

Suddenly, breaking me out of my reverie of watching two old folks being devoured, there was a rap, rap, rappity rap at the snack bar door.

"Bros!" a voice called, "Bros, are you in there?"

It was Judas of course. A fratty lifeguard who came to work hungover sometimes and seemed to subsist on a diet of beer, protein shakes, and double cheeseburgers from the very snack establishment we were currently trapped inside, yet he still had an eight pack of abdominal muscles and pecs that he could jiggle at will.

"Hey Judas," I said cautiously, "You uh, alright?"

Roheed moved towards the door to open it, but I waved for him to stop, awaiting an answer from Judas.

"Of course I'm alright," Judas said, sounding impatient (*hungry* impatient, "hangry" even), "I was just coming to see if you brains were alright."

I cocked my head and looked to Roheed.

Judas laughed, "Heh, heh, I must have brains on the brains. I said brains when I meant… brains."

I sadly shook my head and sliced the air with my hand near my neck in the universal symbol of 'this ain't cuttin' it.'

"Why can't I stop saying brains when I'm clearly trying to say brains?"

You could tell Judas was becoming increasingly aggravated, his speech was becoming slurred, like his tongue was dying from the inside, deep down wherever tongues attach to whatever they're attached to.

There was silence for a bit.

The snack bar back door did actually have a peephole. It was installed so that if the health inspector ever showed up unannounced and knocked on the door some savvy senior manager could see who it was and launch the staff into action, making sure as few health code violations as possible were being perpetrated when the inspector was let in to inspect. I mean, you were always going to be violating a few health codes, technically breathing in the vicinity of food is violating a health code, you just wanted the minimum amount possible for a group of teens and tweens at their first job ever.

Anywho, I crept over to the door and peeked out the peephole. I couldn't see much but the side of the women's locker room and the small grassy area by the front gate and a little piece of the parking lot, where we would park and bring in the boxes of food from our wholesale food warehouse runs.

Out of the corner of the peephole I could actually see my 1989 Plymouth Voyager van, light grey, parked in the Reserved for Snack Bar Manager parking spot.

I was relieved that no zombies or walkers or runners or living dead or brain dead flesh sacks had messed with my ride, and I was about to tell Roheed that the coast was clear, when a single, wide open eye appeared in the peephole and a body *SLAMMED* against the door. I recognized Judas' bloodshot baby blues anywhere.

I scurried away from the door and motioned for Roheed to get back.

"Judas," I said cautiously, "You still OK buddy?"

This time the answer was loud and clear. A guttural roar that was no longer Judas-adjacent came from the thing outside that was no longer Judas. With Roheed's help I pushed the big restaurant-grade double-freezer against the back door.

By the time we sat down on the dirty tile floor, backs against the freezer, drinking bottled water, Former Judas had either tired itself out or moved on to easier-to-eat brains. It was full dark out, and it seemed that we would be spending the night in the snack bar.

The power was still on, so that was a plus. It would have

sucked ass to be trapped in the small, box-like building in the pitch black. Our phones weren't working anymore: no WiFi, no cell service, Twitter's fail whale was holding down the fort on the app with no explanation.

I tried the gas grill, which was working. So I fixed Roheed and I some dinner: burgers and fries and lemonade (we had already taken out the trash, remember, so we couldn't nacho cheese our fries, which was probably a good thing).

We pissed in one of the basins of the big, three basin sink where we did the dishes.

And later we sat on tall stools, looking out the *Order* and the *Pickup* windows, watching the dark silhouettes of our undead neighbors stumble around the pool compound, looking for living flesh to feast upon.

At some point, in the middle of the night things calmed down, there were no new stimuli I guess to rouse the rage within the zombies, so they just kind of milled about. Every once in a while one would splash into the pool or bump into the fence and cause a minor ruckus, but it all became a weird white noise of groans and shuffles so Roheed and I made beds on the floor with sleeves of napkins as pillows and XXL snack bar staff shirts as blankets.

Before we turned off the little orange light over the grill I looked over at Roheed. "Hey," I said, "you alright bud?"

He thought for a moment. "Is this the end?"

"I don't know. Kinda seems like it."

"This is not how I pictured it."

"You're telling me."

"Do you think anyone else survived so far?" he asked.

"They have a pretty good snack bar staff over at the Pointer Ridge pool. I bet a couple of them are doing OK."

Roheed cast his eyes down and couldn't help but smirk in spite of the situation at hand. "Goodnight," he said.

"Night buddy," I said.

At dawn we were wrenched from sleep by an insanely loud buzzing and screaming and the sound of metal cutting rotting flesh. I leapt from my makeshift bed and ran to the *Order* window. Roheed was fast behind me, rubbing some of the Sandman's sandy sleep crystals from his eyes.

That morning we gazed upon quite a sight to see. Jonathan, the Head Lifeguard in Charge, was driving the riding lawn mower to and fro across the swim and racquet club lawn, shuffleboard cue-stick in hand, mowing down the undead left and right. He would ride up on a zombie and corral them into the path of the hungry lawn mower blades with the cue-stick. The bodies would get sucked into the mower mouth and pieces of sheared bone and sliced flesh would spew out the side.

There was a big red jug with holes stabbed in it, pouring gasoline behind him as he went.

He was covered in the black-green blood of the things, viscera clinging to his GUARD polo and red bathing suit shorts. He was yelling a mixture of cowboy colloquialisms like "Yee-haw" and "Get along lil' doggie" and pirate jargon.

"Howdy! Take that ye scurvy landlubber," he shouted as he ran over the top half of a crawler.

I looked to Roheed.

"I'll be right back," I said.

Roheed's eyes shot open, the caramel of his eye surrounded by white, like a reverse caramel cream candy that we sold in the snack bar for 25 cents each.

"No!" he said, knowing what I was about to do.

I was already rolling the fridge away from the back door. "Stay by the door and uh, grab one of those chef's knives. Don't let me in if I say 'brains' more than once in a sentence."

Before I unlocked the door I looked back to Roheed.

"You're an excellent assistant manager, 'Heed."

And with that I left the safety of the snack bar, a long grill fork in one hand and a plastic tray like a shield in the other.

The next few moments felt like hours, I moved in slow motion. I slammed the door shut behind me and I heard the latch lock with a deafening cuh-*CLACK*. I ran to the edge of the top deck, to the fence with the chipped green painted metal bars. I stood up on the middle bar and waved my arms at Jonathan.

"Jonathan!" I yelled. "Jonathan! Me and Roheed are alive too!"

Jonathan obviously couldn't hear me over the clamor of the machinery he was piloting, but he got the gist. He turned the steering wheel and started heading my way. We both had big ole' grins on our faces at the sight of a fellow breather.

Jonathan saw it before me, he was about half-way between the pump house and the snack bar, pretty much near the flag pole. No one had raised the flag that morning. When he noticed he tried to tell me, but again, the engine of his mower and the whirring of the blades underneath were too loud for me to hear. And I was caught up in watching him, as the handful of zombies that were still on the pool grounds followed him. It seemed they had turned from the lackadaisical *Shaun Of The Dead* type to more of the Zack Snyder *Dawn Of The Dead* runners once Jonathan had started slaughtering them and the blood was in the air.

But anyway, Jonathan saw that the thing that used to be Judas was sneaking up behind me. Or hobbling rather, as sometime in the night it must have lost a leg somehow. But nonetheless it was hop-dragging towards me and I was none the wiser. In fact, I didn't know until its fangs chomped down on my Achilles tendon. Then I was aware of its presence, that's for sure. It felt like flames shot up from the bite, but when I looked down there was no fire, just the Judas-thing retracting its jaws from my leg, poised to take another mouthful from my ankle.

I stabbed it in the butt with my grill fork and hopped out of its bite radius, then stomped down on its skull with the bit leg. It hurt like a raging bitch, but the crunch of the zombie's now-softened, but still crispy skull, was satisfying as hell.

Jonathan finally made it over to me and pulled me up onto the lawnmower and we rode over the Judas zombie. Its blood showered us. I rubbed the gunk out of my eyes and ears. We hopped off of the mower and pounded on the snack bar back door.

"Roheed!" I yelled. "Let us in. I probably still have a little time."

Roheed opened the door and regarded me warily. Jonathan nodded to him to let us in and he did.

I lay in the back of the snack bar with my leg elevated, ice pack on the festering wound where I was bit. Black tendrils of sickness spread from the jagged teeth marks. I didn't have much time left, but damn it, I was still going to R.I.C.E. (rest, ice, compress, elevate) my injury while I could.

"So you holed up in the guard office overnight?" I asked Jonathan, through gritted teeth, trying to keep the boiling water of consciousness in my brain from bubbling over into insanity.

"Yeah," he said, "I stayed the night there, uh, just last night. That's the only time I ever did that."

Roheed just paced in the front of the snack shack, wringing his hands.

"I noticed a lull this morning and I snuck over to the pump house to get the riding lawn mower and some gasoline and… I guess the rest is history."

I upturned my clenched jaw into the only version of a smile I could muster. "That was the best thing I'll see in my life."

Jonathan just smiled and toweled my brow.

I nodded to my keys, "Take 'em. Find whoever else is out there. Roheed, take some food."

Roheed thrived on direction and quickly got to work.

"It was fun working with you Jon," I said.

Jonathan smiled, "It was fun working with you too. Thanks for all the free food."

"Don't mention it."

I had Roheed fry me up one last order of mozzarella

sticks, which I ate, even though my taste for food was already gone. In fact, the marinara that I dunked them in was kind of a tease. I kept hoping the thick tomato-y sauce would be warmer and saltier... and taste like human blood.

I created a diversion as Roheed and Jonathan climbed out of the *Pickup* window onto the roof, then hopped over the fence onto the old cardboard box stack that hadn't been taken for recycling yet (and never would?) and got into my van and drove off. I made it to the riding lawn mower, my brain starting to fog, and made enough noise and I guess I still had enough of that "heart-beatin' smell" that drives the zombies wild. And they followed me as I rode the mower, pouring the rest of the gas behind me as I went, towards the flagpole and the pump house and beyond.

My very last thought was that I felt like it would be nice to take a look at the view of the pool from the high dive one last time. I probably hadn't been up there in a good five or so summers, and I remembered it was always a thrill. So I used the lighter that we kept in the snack bar in case the pilot light on the grill ever went out to light the gas soaked rag I had stuffed into the gas tank of the mower, and walked away as the mower exploded, burning up a couple brain-eaters, and sending shrapnel into the bodies of several others.

I was pretty sure one of the blades from the mower had lodged itself in my back as I climbed the scritchy-scratchy black grip tape covered ladder, up to the high diving board, but it didn't bother me. I wasn't feeling pain anymore per se, just an unfathomable hunger that I hadn't ever felt before.

The view from up there was exquisite. A soft wind rippled through the tall trees. Bodies of both regular dead and undead bobbed around in the pool. And smoke billowed up from the bombed out mower that had set the gasoline soaked grass and wooden picnic tables ablaze. Plastic blue and white striped deck chairs melted.

I took my last deep breath. Struggled on my bad leg to create enough momentum to give a little hop on the wobbly tip of the board, bounced once, and let the board send me up, then gravity pull me down towards the murky water.

A smile crawled its way across my now pale green lips and I said "Cannon... brains!"

School For The Sleepless

by Andrew Adams

I NEVER SHOULD have taken the job.

It must have been back in '72, and I'd never worked a day in my life. There were no ads, mind you. No classifieds that said: *Help Wanted*. Dr. Mortimer Mills didn't invite the scrutiny, see? Oh, no. Prying eyes weren't welcome at all, not at the Institute.

Now, I don't know what deal he struck with the devil to keep his students in such isolation, but the world at large seemed to know that they would not be welcomed inside. Maybe it was the way his school was near impossible to track down, tucked so deep into Appalachia that nobody even knew which state borders it resided in or which authorities might have jurisdiction there. I always thought maybe Maryland but my cousin, he swears it was West Virginia. A two-story cement trap built God knows when, without one single window (better to hide the secrets within).

I arrived in October, I remember, cause there was a chill in the air. It was daytime, sure, but you couldn't tell. The brown leaves were so dense in every direction that even the sun seemed unwelcome. And I was walking up through the woods, to the brick building with my bags in hand, past the sign that said *School For The Sleepless*...

That's when I noticed the shapes.

The people, all in the woods.

Wandering aimless, like a horde of undead. Moaning and moving half-speed, leering with their bloodshot eyes, jaws slacked open and drooling.

The insomniacs.

A haunting sight, but I needed the job. That job precisely. So I kept walking up that path, ignoring the red eyes all around me, the sound of shuffling footsteps stumbling among the brush, and I went up to the knob. I turned it.

And I entered the dark.

Sometimes, still, I wish that I hadn't. And let it be a lesson that you always trust your gut. I should have turned back, should have known how wrong it all was when I saw those depraved and weary faces. It's not like I needed the money, or had a burning unmet passion to do janitorial work. Not at all. But it was the only way that I could think to get in there.

The only way to learn why my brother disappeared.

His name was Jonny. Or is Jonny, I don't know. He might be alive. And his problems all began on the night he turned thirteen.

It was after the cake and after the presents and after all the puberty jokes, after I teased him for his weirdly big ears (a new development). It was after the family had all fallen asleep.

Even me. Warm in bed. Alone in my room.

So I thought.

But it was his scream that woke me, a bloodcurdling cackle that cracked on its way out of his throat, and I woke up and saw him standing at the head of my bed, his curly hair unkempt in a way that looked like horns.

Then he bent down and bit my neck.

Now I love Jonny, you gotta know. Always have, always will. He was the courageous little brother (and me: the shy older sister). I was never as brave. Never willing to climb so high, or to speak my mind. Completely unable to step foot in the woods behind our house, with all its weird shapes and shadows looming in the treetops, unable to follow him when he'd run in to play with friends I'd never met. But whenever I protested, he'd come back and stay behind. For me.

The good brother.

I was confused when his teeth broke my skin. I hit him hard and he fell back and he cracked his head open wide on the edge of my dresser, a deep bloody gash that went right across the full width of his forehead, which caused him to tumble into a corner and ask: "How did I get here?"

He was sleepwalking, see, and we both paid the price. Wound up with matching scars to mark the occasion. His on his forehead, jagged as a star, and mine in a circle on the side of my neck.

When the blood was cleaned and the sun was risen and we were all at the table trying to make sense of what happened, Jonny looked down (so ashamed) and said in his cracking, creaking voice: "Is this gonna happen again?"

"I hope not," said Momma.

"But your body *is* changing," said Poppa.

And I asked: "Why the heck did you bite my neck?"

He simply shrugged and got sheepish and whispered: "I dreamt I was Dracula."

When I arrived at the School For The Sleepless for my job orientation, I was greeted by the doctor's assistant. A decrepit old woman named Miriam, with wrinkled skin and rotting gums that took up most of her mouth (so that even when she smiled, all I saw was decay). She wore dark gloves and an all-black habit that ran from her crooked jaw down to her ankles. Her fashion, it seemed, was a century old.

"The Institute is two stories," she said, her voice slow and full of effort. "Children live on the top and learn down below. But we keep it dark all day, so that students can sleep if their body allows it. Dr. Mills believes that it's best to let nature progress unimpeded."

She led me up a spiral staircase and onto the second floor, a long concrete hall that seemed to stretch into infinite. The air was wet, dank, and chilly.

Like a cave.

There were open doors every twenty feet and dozens and dozens of insomniacs, out of their rooms and overrunning the hall. All in tattered bathrobes, as if ready for sleep at a second's notice. They seemed dazed, listless, and somber. One young boy leaned against a wall with his back turned, silent as stone. Two teenage girls stood side-by-side, chewing on one another's hair. And another boy shuffled (sighing) down the hall, occasionally stopping to pick up a beetle or spider and pop it into his mouth.

I wanted to gag.

Miriam beamed. "You can see why we need a new cleaner," she said. Motioning toward the walls, which were painted with a sterile green paint that was now peeling and crawling with bugs.

We passed through the swarm of sleepless students, past bedroom after bedroom. Then, I noticed there were no *beds* in those bedrooms. Just hooks hanging up on the walls.

"Where do they sleep?" I asked.

She said, "They don't."

We all hoped that Jonny's sleepwalking was a one-time occurrence, but it became as routine as the moon, with its near nightly schedule.

A cute charming brother all day.

A mean little monster all night.

I learned to lock my doors. But still, every hour that I sought slumber, I'd hear my doorknob rattle and shake.

We started tying him down, to no avail. In his sleepwalking state he could still outsmart us at every stage, bypassing doors and undoing knots and appearing in every corner we looked, like nothing could keep him down. As if he could somehow squeeze through the cracks and the seams of our house.

He attacked me three more times. Never on purpose, not even half-conscious. But it became too much, and it started to change us. Made me paranoid and unhappy, made him sad and dejected and all filled with guilt. We could feel the trust shifting inside us, slipping away, until even in the daytime all I could think about was who I'd meet at night.

And then, after a yelling match where I told him I thought we'd all be better off if he just dropped dead, he stopped sleeping at all.

Sometimes I wonder if this is all my fault.

We found him the next morning with his eyes pink, staring in a daze out the window, and every time his head nodded off he would slap himself gently and perk back up.

"Honey, please, you have to sleep," said Momma.

"I don't wanna hurt you," he said. "Not anymore."

And that's how it went, for days and weeks. We'd retire to bed and Jonny would exit the house, run through the woods like a feral child, and any time he felt his eyes start to droop he'd do something wild to wake himself up. He started speaking delirious nonsense, would flinch and react to sounds no one could hear, and told us tales of new friends in the woods. I could see him slipping away.

And then, one night, there was a knock on the door. Momma opened it up and out on the porch stood the tallest, thinnest man I've ever met. Gaunt and pale like a stick, with long white hair slicked all the way back to his shoulders, fingers like praying mantis claws, wearing a three-piece suit made of purple velvet. His eyes were pale and ghostly (half-coated with cataracts). Just his being there seemed to suck all the warmth out of the room, and I felt my stomach ache.

"My name is Dr. Mortimer Mills," he said. "And I hear your son has a condition."

As my tour of the school progressed, I noticed a scratching sound behind the walls.

"What is *that?*" I asked, noticing that I could hear it all through the halls.

"Oh." Ancient Mrs. Miriam stopped, seemingly debating whether to tell me. When she spoke again, it felt like half-truth. "Don't worry. The School for the Sleepless was built on top of a cave system. Sometimes the sound travels upwards."

And then I felt hands. Grabbing my body.

It was one of the insomniacs stumbling through the hall.

A girl, age unknown but maybe late teens, hair tangled around her wide-open eyes, and she slammed me against the wall and she screamed, *"Run!"*

I should have listened.

"Lilith!" shouted Miriam. "Stop that!"

But the girl looked me right in the eyes and I knew, for

the first time but not the last, what pure panic looks like. Her face contorted into a sorrowful howl, the muscles on her face knotting in agony, and when she spoke it was almost a hiss, droplets of spit flying onto my cheeks.

"Help me!"

"Grab her!" Miriam commanded nearby boys to run in, to grab this girl (Lilith) and to pull her (kicking, fighting) down toward the end of the hall. They were moving fast but I ran to keep up, and I saw Miriam reach into her habit and pull out a heavy iron ring full of skeleton keys, jingling in her hand as she hurried ahead of the rest.

"Help me!" cried Lilith. "Help!"

The sleepless boys pulled the screaming girl down a set of uneven stone stairs that led to a heavy wooden door, which Miriam pulled open with an ear-splitting groan. The door was massive, unlike anything else in the school, and led into shadow. But Miriam waved everyone onward and the boys pulled Lilith in.

"Don't let them change me! *Don't let them change me!*" she yelled.

Miriam ignored Lilith and slammed the door shut with a heavy, resounding bang, which echoed into the halls and made my ears sting.

The old woman moved fast, drawing chains down over the doors and closing padlocks and using her keys to seal it all shut, ensuring no one else would follow.

I heard Lilith's screams fade away as she was dragged beyond the door. I wondered what horrors lay beyond it. And if Jonny already knew.

Then Miriam turned to me and smiled. Putting her keys away.

"Don't let that disturb you," she said, stepping back up the stairs. I shrunk away and she sensed the fear. She backed me into a corner, up against the wall, and put her hand on my shoulder. "The sleepless are an unpredictable sort, as a mind without rest is prone to paranoia. Don't believe what anyone says here. Everyone lies."

I had no doubt.

When the Doctor entered our house that night, he stood absolutely still.

"Would you like to sit?" asked Momma. But he said no.

"I'm a headmaster," said Dr. Mills. "At the School For The Sleepless. We specialize in raising children whose... natural habits do not conform to the rest of the world's. We feed them, we house them, and we teach them all they need to know. So that they can grow into the absolute *best* versions of themselves." He scanned the room, moving only his eyes, and locked in on me. Then smiled. "How about you, little girl? Do *you* sleep?"

I'm not little.

"It's just our boy," said Poppa. "Jonny, c'mere!"

There was a thump from the far room. And then, soon after, Jonny dragged himself into the room at half-speed, out of energy. His eyes seemed to wobble in his skull, completely unable to focus. "Master," he said, with the dullest of bows.

"*Headmaster,*" said Momma.

And then Dr. Mills moved (finally), bending forward until he came eye-to-eye with my brother. "Hello, Jonny," he said. "Would you like to be where you belong?"

Jonny winced and turned away. Ever since his insomnia started, he was overly sensitive to sound.

"He hasn't had rest in more than a month," said Momma.

"Can you fix him?" asked Poppa.

And the Doctor rose again. He took a deep breath, looked us all in the eyes (one-by-one). And then he spoke. "I don't believe that your boy is broken. What I see here is untapped potential, and I do not want to squash it. My school will *foster* this new phase of development, so that Jonny can become his true self. One with the night… Where he thrives."

Jonny hadn't moved.

And the Doctor whispered, "What do you think, Jonny? Are you ready to *soar?*"

I spent that first week searching the school, looking for any sign of my brother. The job was a perfect cover. As long as I carried a mop nobody seemed to question what room I was in. But he was nowhere to be found.

The sleepless students scared me but I knew they had answers, so I tried to be like Jonny.

Brave, be brave.

I worked up the nerve to pull them aside and ask if they'd heard of my brother ("He's the boy in this picture, with the star-shaped scar on his head!"). But they never knew, or they didn't remember, or maybe all of them lied.

The sleepless didn't express their emotions any way that you or I would. Sometimes they'd hiss at my questions, baring their teeth like beasts. Other times they opened their mouth but no sound came out. And none of them looked in my eyes. Few seemed to use sight at all, walking the halls with their eyes closed (in some place halfway between wake and slumber), navigating the grounds as if by sixth sense.

I wondered what was behind that heavy wooden door, the one the boys had dragged Lilith into. Whatever had happened to Jonny, I knew I'd find it there.

But how to get into it without those keys?

And then he came for me.

Dr. Mills.

I jumped when he walked through my door, taller and bonier than I remembered. Dressed in his velvet suit, with a scowl on his face. He stared at me for too long and my whole body shook, wondering what ran through his mind. It was the first time I'd seen him in the building, and I worried that he'd remember me from that day in my home. That he'd know I was the sister of a missing boy and that I hadn't come for the job.

Then he curled one finger and said: "I need you. Now."

He didn't say a single other word as we walked through the halls.

Every footstep felt like a death march.

We got closer and closer to his private office.

He stopped when we approached his door, tall and heavy and windowless, and he took out his own set of skeleton keys. My heart skipped a beat.

There they were.

My best chance to get through the door downstairs, into the darkness, to maybe (*maybe!*) find Jonny.

Then he thrust open the door and he pulled me in with those overlong fingers and I wanted to gag in an instant.

The smell of his office was putrid and sour.

Because of the bats.

There were hundreds, maybe thousands, of bats. Swarming (*everywhere*), all over the room. Hanging upside down off the ceiling, the lamps, the chairs, the shelves. Bunched up so thick that they blacked out the walls, made the ceiling seem like a river (a rippling and bubbling undulating ooze). They were loud (so loud), flapping and shrieking and clicking and clawing. Big ones, orange ones, brown and small and snaggletoothed ones, ones with ugly collections of uneven (extra) flesh dangling off their faces, black membranous wings and veins and little glints of white ivory fangs (blades!) and lolling red tongues.

"*Clean,*" he said.

And he pointed to the corner, where a bucket and brush were waiting. I noticed that the floors were covered in a white gooey substance and it hit me all at once. The smell. The *guano*. The colony's waste dripping on every surface. Disgusting.

He crossed to his desk. He seemed completely unafraid of the bats swirling around him. The creatures navigated his office with ease, zipping around him and his desk and his antique chairs and then launching their little black bodies (full of disease) down into a dark hole in the ground, chiseled into stone, and I saw that this was no infestation, no unwanted vermin.

Dr. Mills had drilled a hole directly down into the caves below.

Inviting these monsters in.

I stood there frozen, and he slammed his heavy keys down on his desk and said: "Do your *job*, girl." And then he stopped and he squinted, putting his long hands on his desk and leaning forward. Bats, as if trained, flew to his shoulders, digging their tiny claws into his jacket.

And he said: "I know you."

My throat got hard and I wanted to panic.

I could see him connecting the dots.

But I willed myself: *be brave (like Jonny).*

"It's not my first day," I said. And I dropped to my knees, put them right in the waste that covered the floor, and I started to scrub up the bat discharge with bare hands. Trying hard to look committed, like I loved to clean, with or without my gloves. I felt goop in my fingers.

He seemed satisfied. "Yes. Yes. I suppose that's it."

He sat down. A bat on his shoulder hissed in anger.

I continued to scrub.

"No noise while I work," he said.

I slowed my pace. I remember staying that way for many minutes, trying to know what to do. I wanted those keys. Wanted to see what was hidden below. Wanted to find my brother. But I didn't want to upset him, and I was scared of his bats. They consumed my thoughts (why would he *like* this?!) and every time one dropped from the ceiling and spread its wings to return down below I would seize up and my arms would bubble with goosebumps.

But I developed a plan.

I started scrubbing (slowly, softly) closer and closer toward his desk.

Closer and closer toward his keys.

And it was all going well until I felt a hairy little creature land on my neck, a bat twice the size of my head, and I screamed (on instinct) and I swiveled and I started to slap, trying to knock it away, but Dr. Mills leapt to his feet with his eyes flaring wide and he lunged for my wrist and yanked me forward hard enough to pin me down on his desk (so hard that it hurt) and he *screamed* in my ear as loud as he could: "No. *No!*"

Bats screeched, matching his volume, and then he raised one hand and I flinched away from the impact but he seemed to take two breaths, reconsider, his body shaking in anger but his mind exerting control, and then he said: "Don't be scared of these beautiful creatures."

He let go. I backed away.

And he looked all around him, at the roomful of bats. "We are surrounded by miracles," he said. "They perceive the world in ways we could not fathom. They *see* sound! And they live ten times longer than any other creature their size. They are a sacred pinnacle of evolution and I will *not* have you harm them!"

The room went quiet.

As if these bats deferred to a master.

Then I shivered and sighed and I said, "I'm sorry."

"Get out!" he screamed. "You'll finish tomorrow!"

And I ran as fast as I could. Out of his door and into the hall but not back to my room. No. I ran all the way down (sprinting, sprinting) until I hit that big wooden door, and then I pulled his keys out of my pocket.

I had grabbed them when he shoved me onto his desk.

My hands shook so hard that I could barely open the lock.

But I did, and the door creaked and it groaned and it opened before me.

Revealing a twisted set of dark steps leading down into darkness below.

I started forward. Desperately hoping to find my brother.

My parents turned down the doctor that night he arrived on our doorstep, wisely unwilling to send their only son away with a stranger.

But his offer lingered in everyone's mind...

Like a plague.

Jonny's condition got worse. He said that his head always

hurt and the world was full of noise. He held conversations with shadows and spent more nights wandering the woods beyond our house, stumbling through those tall, thick trees that I found so imposing, that the older kids in town said were so full of monsters. He'd come back in the mornings with cuts and scratches.

He never seemed happy.

And then, eventually, it was Jonny who made the plea.

"Please. *Please!* I have to go!" he screamed, waking us all up in the middle of the night. "I don't *belong* here!" He had his eyes shut and was shouting out of an open window, howling to be heard. We hoped he was talking to us, but looking back I know that's not the case. I know now that he was speaking to his friends in the trees. *"Please just take me there!"*

In the morning, Jonny was gone.

My parents panicked. Police were called. But there was no trace of Jonny, no hint as to how he went missing or where he could be. Just an empty bed in the morning light. The investigation into Dr. Mills and his School For The Sleepless was cursory at best. There was no real evidence that Jonny had been there.

But I knew it in my heart.

I knew he'd found a way.

Which is how I wound up running down those dark steps, Dr. Mills' keys in my hand, moving past that ancient wooden door and traveling down, down, deeper down still.

My heart was pounding. I leapt over steps, moving two, three, sometimes four at a time. I could hear flapping wings draw near. The light fell away and I had to press my hand against the wall for guidance. Wondering when Dr. Mills would notice his missing keys. Hoping to find whatever lay beneath before he could catch me.

Down. Down.

Into darkness.

And soon I heard screams.

A girl's voice, echoing up through the stairwell. Not far away. And even though I'd only heard her once, I knew the sound. It was Lilith. The girl they dragged away. Could Jonny be with her?

"Where'd you go?!" It was Dr. Mills, at the top of the steps. Yelling, in rage, his voice like a dagger. His footsteps echoed as he hurried after me. "This room is not for *you!*"

All the more reason to see it.

I followed the screams until I saw flickering torchlight, bouncing off the moldy, stony walls, and I came off the steps and into a massive cavern.

I stood in a giant stone amphitheater lit by dozens of

torches, casting an orange hue over jagged stalactites. There were rock columns fifty feet tall and shimmering calcite growths sheeting the walls.

And there, in the center of the cave, was Lilith.

Chained to the ground, heavy iron shackles on her wrists and her ankles keeping her down, and her body was covered in vermin. The bats. Crawling along her flesh, biting and feeding and drawing blood. As if they would eat her alive.

"No!" I screamed, running to help her.

But Dr. Mills pulled me back.

"Do *not* interfere," he said.

I turned and saw him behind me, sneering and mad. I reacted on impulse, swinging a fist up and into his chest, but he grabbed my wrist to stop me.

So much stronger than his thin frame appeared.

"What are you *doing?!*" I screamed. "You're letting them kill her!"

"No," he said. "You misunderstand."

And then he dragged me by the wrist, pulling me closer to Lilith, and he put his overlong fingers around the back of my neck and pushed me close to her face. Letting me see.

She was no longer human.

Her ears had grown into points and the skin on her face was starting to sag and to stretch, reshaping and reforming into new folds and structures. Her teeth had sharpened into little blades and new flesh was being produced under her arms, pink and translucent and connecting her limbs to her torso. Like wings.

"What are you *doing* to her?" I asked.

"Nothing," said the Doctor. "This is a natural step in human evolution."

He went to the creature I once knew as Lilith and she clicked and screeched.

Like his bats.

"It's a marvelous thing," he said. "If you want to soar through the skies, to gain new sight, to live ten times as long... Then this is the way. It starts when hearing enhances, which makes it hard to sleep. And then it leads to so much more." He was looking at the half-formed creature before him with what could only be envy and admiration. "If our culture didn't do all in its power to stamp out the people they deem different, then maybe we would all be so lucky."

Lilith nuzzled her face into his knuckles.

"Is this what happens to... *all* insomniacs?" I asked.

"I hope so," he said.

He let me go later that night. He said he had nothing to hide and no reason to stop me. But if I ever caused any trouble, if

I ever stood in the way of human evolution, then he'd send his friends in the forest to stop me. He warned: they'd be watching.

I never found Jonny, not for sure. But when I returned home (and into Momma and Poppa's relieved embrace), I continued to search. After all I'd seen in the School For The Sleepless, the woods behind our house ceased to scare me. I began to explore them, night after night, tracing Jonny's footsteps. Hoping one day I'd find him.

Soon I heard voices.

And saw the shapes in the treetops.

I realized that they'd been there all along. Shadowy figures perched on the highest branches, watching me with the blood-red eyes of insomniacs. Dozens, always all around, always watching. Out of my sight.

"Have any of you seen my brother?" I asked one night.

And one of the creatures lifted its long, sinewy limbs and launched into the air, letting the wind catch its wings. It seemed four feet tall while hunching on branches but was much bigger in flight, and it soared down through the dark forest until it landed before me. A new phase of evolution, half-bat and half-human, further developed than Lilith was when I saw her. And then this strange, hideous creature waddled forward and opened its wings wide and wrapped me inside them.

I saw it had a star-shaped scar on its forehead.
Needless to say, I haven't slept since.

Fangirl

by Beck Medina

RICK

"So... here it is. My apartment," Mandy says, my hand in hers as she steps over the creaky wooden floor of her two story Pasadena townhouse.

My first impression is that it's small, but charming. A lot like Mandy. Everything, from the beige paint on the walls to the scratched up furniture, is old and worn. It's like a fixer upper that she never got to work on fixing up.

An embarrassed smile crosses over Mandy's face when she catches me checking out her place. "I know it probably isn't what you're used to, Mr. Rockstar."

I drop my jaw. I can't believe she's pulling that card on me. Now I'm the one who's embarrassed.

"Hey, watch it," I say, pointing an index finger at her, but smiling. "I like it. I think it's great. Charlie Monroe owns property in a neighborhood out here. He was telling me all about it the last time I hung out with him. We share a manager."

Ugh, I only realize after I've spoken how douchey I must sound. It's easy to talk like this with my brothers or our friends in the business. But to a girl like Mandy? She told me she works in music but I doubt she wants to hear about my celebrity friends. Lord knows I wouldn't want to if I was her.

"Can I let you in on a secret?" Mandy says as she removes her jacket. She bites her lower lip, and it's bright, pearly whites against the deep red of her lipstick. It's kind of sexy. "Charlie Monroe is kind of the reason I rent this place."

I widen my mouth into a big grin. "You really are a fangirl, aren't you?"

"I'm trying to keep my cool."

"I think you're very cool," I say, stepping over to Mandy and embracing her. I plant a kiss on her neck. "And sexy. Tonight has been a blast. I'm glad you came up to me."

Mandy shoots a smirk at me. Damn, she is hot. I place my hand on the back of her dark hair to pull her in for a kiss. Her lips are soft, but aggressive. When I pull away, we're both breathing a little heavier than before.

"You live here all by yourself?" I say, still holding her tight.

"I sure do." Mandy sweeps her arms out from my grip and rests them around my shoulders. "I was offered my tour promotions job right out of high school this past summer. Don't *you* live by yourself?"

I think I might be blushing. I peer down and clear my throat like that will conceal it. "My brothers and I live with our parents."

Mandy tilts her head to the side. "Awww."

"Yeah, yeah, yeah," I say, but she's already eating it up. I can't tell if Mandy finds it cute, or if she actually is poking fun of me.

I get it, though. It *is* kind of weird that a guy like me would be living with my parents. My band *The Spiral Dragons* sells out stadium shows. Our albums have all gone multi-platinum. And I'm about to turn nineteen. I *should* be living in some lavish mansion by myself.

But there's a good reason why I don't. When I turned eighteen last year I moved into a place out in Sherman Oaks with my older brother Adam. That was when the success of our band was first picking up momentum. Things change, though. And fast. Tragedy has a way of sneaking in and shaking things up.

Mandy lets out a long sigh. "Rick Jerry. Standing in my living room after his big stadium show. It almost feels too good to be true."

"I can be Rick Jerry: Standing In Your Bedroom if you'd like."

Mandy scoffs at this, but I can tell she's loving where this is going. She releases me and strolls over to the kitchen. "How about something to drink first?"

"Sure," I say, and let her disappear into the kitchen to fix something up for us.

I remove my coat and fold it, uncertain for a second where I should put it. I don't want to be rude.

"You can leave your stuff on the couch," Mandy calls, like she can see what's going on. "I'll take care of it when I'm done."

"I can put it somewhere if you want," I volunteer, walking over to a door that I'm assuming must be the coat closet. I reach for the knob and start to open the door.

"No!" Mandy slams her hand into the door. It closes right away. She must see that I'm taken aback, because she smiles and waves off the door. "That thing is a damn mess. Your drink," she says, handing me a glass of tequila with club soda. "I remember you're diabetic."

I smile at this. I've never gone home with a fan before. That was always more up my brother Adam's alley. But there was something about Mandy that told me I needed to leave the after party with her.

While I'm sipping on my drink, Mandy gives me a walk-through of the entire downstairs of her place. There isn't a whole lot to see, but it's nice that she's doing all the talking.

I'm starting to get tired and it's gotta be like one a.m. at this point. I haven't looked at my phone since we got in our Uber.

"You've been to our show before," I say, pointing to a photo she has framed on the wall of ticket stubs from our last tour.

"A while back, yeah," she says, and wraps her arms around her chest.

"It's too bad we didn't meet."

"I wasn't as hot back then, so…" Mandy glances at me. "Wanna see the upstairs now?"

When we get to her bedroom I've already finished my drink. I give the glass a shake and peer inside to make sure it's empty.

"You can set it on the nightstand," she tells me without even looking. I swear this girl's got eyes in the back of her head. It feels like she knows exactly what I'm doing at all times, she's so aware of her surroundings.

"What's this collection you have here?" I say, walking over to the little console table in front of her bedroom window.

It's a whole collection of little anime looking dolls, but I recognize exactly who they are. They're pop stars. Charlie Monroe, Tyler Brooks, Danny De La Cruz. All guys in bands. Their skin is realistic and soft to the touch with big, sad looking anime eyes and a little line for a mouth. I practically shudder when my finger grazes little Charlie Monroe's shiny, dark and curly hair. It feels lifelike.

But there's one doll that really catches my eye. I'm entranced by it even.

I pick up the doll and take a good look at it. "This looks just like my brother."

"I hope you don't think it's weird that I have your brother," Mandy says, half serious, half joking. "My goal is to collect them all. These dolls are hard to get. They're worth a lot."

I let out an easy laugh. "Not at all. I get it. You're a fan."

I just can't believe I'm looking into his hazel eyes again. I know they're not really his eyes, but...

"What's it been like? Since your brother's been gone?"

Adam went missing over a year ago. Nobody ever found his body, but we know he's dead. He left a party one night after our show and we never heard from him again. Kyle, our eldest brother, and I figured he was going to hook up with a girl. He'd done it before. Many times. We thought nothing of it until he didn't return home the next morning. At first we thought he was just smitten by this one. Adam *always* came back.

"Tough." I finally say. "It still doesn't feel real sometimes. You know, I used to get these phone calls around the time he disappeared. I'd get a call from some unknown number and there would be silence on the other line. I don't know why but, I had a feeling it was him. Like he was contacting me from the dead."

I laugh, aware of how crazy this all must sound. I don't even know why I'm sharing it to begin with. Only my therapist knows this stuff.

Mandy places her hand on my shoulder. I feel comforted immediately. "What if he's not dead, though? What if he's just... needing to get away for a while or something? Maybe fame got to him?"

I shake my head. "Adam would never leave us. Not suddenly like that. Something bad happened to him."

Mandy frowns. I know she's trying to help, but she's killing the mood. Trust me, the last thing she wants is for me to go into dark and brooding mode. I don't want to be depressed tonight. That's why I came here to begin with.

I set the doll back with the others and turn to Mandy. I won't be looking at these things for the rest of the night. Or ever again for that matter.

"Show me something else?" I suggest, letting my words linger a bit.

"How about... the bed?"

I raise my brows. "Good idea."

I doubt we've been asleep for long when suddenly I wake. I shoot my eyes open and feel my face. Everything seems to be intact. Plus, my heart is beating like I just ran a marathon. I'm definitely alive.

Mandy's got her back to me, and the steadiness of her breath as her shoulders rise up and down tell me that she's sound asleep.

It must have been a crazy dream. I've never dreamt that lucidly before.

But then a giant thud echoes throughout the room so loud that I'm surprised Mandy doesn't wake up.

I sit up in bed, peering around the room to find the culprit. There isn't anything on the floor. Aside from our clothes, the creamy white carpet is clean.

I lay back down and close my eyes, giving sleep another go. I'm just not used to sleeping in someone else's house. Not since Adam's disappearance. It's something I need to readjust to. That's all.

"Rick…" a voice whispers.

I shoot my eyes open.

What.

The.

HELL!?

That's Adam's voice. I feel the tears forming in my eyes from the disbelief. I haven't heard that voice in so long. Yes,

I've rewatched old videos and interviews and have heard Adam's voice, but this was *here*. In the room. Without a screen between us.

"Rick…" the voice calls again, like it's a part of the night breeze.

I turn my head, and sitting on a chair on my side of the room is Adam's doll.

I scream.

This wakes Mandy. She jolts out of bed and throws her arms up.

"Jesus!" she says, tightening her hands into fists when she realizes it was me who screamed. "You scared the hell out of me! What's the matter with you?"

"Adam… I mean, that doll… moved." I point to the doll seated in the chair as it looks back at us. "It was over there." I point to the collection of dolls across from us, then to the chair. "And now it's there."

This amuses Mandy. "Awww. Are you afraid of dolls, Rick?"

"I'm afraid of this one. I mean, I'm not afraid of it. I just… could we move it to a different room?"

Mandy bites her lip to withhold her laughter. "Of course. Be right back." She throws the covers off her and crosses over to the doll. She picks it up, holding it carefully with both hands, then wanders out of the bedroom.

I wipe my palms across my face. Am I seriously shaken up over a little doll? To be fair, the doll looks exactly like my dead brother. It was created intentionally to *be* him, in doll form. But there's just no way. Unless Mandy's playing some kind of weird prank on me. No, she couldn't be. She's been asleep this whole time.

Mandy passes by in the hallway. "Bathroom," she says when we make eye contact, and she keeps on walking.

Is that doll out there? Unattended? Am I *really* afraid of it?

I get out of bed and start for the kitchen. I need a drink.

I make another tequila with club soda from what I can find in Mandy's kitchen. I take a sip and exhale a big breath, then I lean against the counter.

"Rick?"

"Ah!" I scream and turn around. Doll Adam is seated on the counter right where I just was.

"Shhhhh," I hear Adam say. The doll's mouth isn't moving, but Adam's voice *is* coming from it. This is impossible.

"Pipe down, you idiot," he says.

"You talk?" I throw my hands on my head hysterically. "What is happening?"

"Be quiet or you'll wake her! I'm not trying to hurt you, Rick. I'm trying to *help* you. You have to get out of here."

I narrow my eyes. "Why? She's giving me a ride to the

airport tomorrow morning and she lives in *Pasadena*. She's a keeper as far as I'm concerned. *You're* the problem, here! You don't... exist!" I point an accusing finger at Doll Adam.

"She's not who she says she is. You need to leave."

"And *you* need to chill. Wait..." I let out a laugh. I think I'm experiencing an epiphany. "I'm having an imaginary conversation with a doll who's made to look like my brother. I need to go back to Doctor Michelle."

I wonder if Doctor Michelle has any availability for when I get back from the UK. She'll have a field day when she hears about this newly formed insanity I'm serving. I reach into the pocket of my jeans for my phone, but it's gone. I feel the outsides of all my pockets. Huh. I must have left my phone in my jacket pocket when I first got here. I'll have to check later.

"So I'm going to head back to bed. This conversation is over. I don't talk to inanimate objects. You're not real."

I turn my back away from the doll, ready to walk away when Adam says, "I came home with Mandy. Just like you."

I freeze and return to face Doll Adam. "When?"

"The night I disappeared. Where do you think I've *been* this whole time?"

I widen my eyes. "Dead! Are you saying you're a... a doll?"

"Don't believe me? Check the closet."

"What closet?" I wait for an answer, but Adam doesn't

respond. I shake my head and pace around the kitchen counter. "No, no. This can't be real. You're just a figment of my obviously damaged brain! I'm not over your death, Adam. Please, just get out of here!"

Mandy crosses into the kitchen, her brows furrowed. I'm sure I must seem crazy to her. I'd think the same if I were in her shoes.

"Everything OK in here?"

I turn toward Doll Adam, but he's gone. He really needs to stop doing that. I'm about to have a panic attack.

"Yeah. Just... had a nightmare. It's been a weird night for my brain."

Mandy laughs lightly. She makes her way to the stove and lifts the tea kettle from the burner it rests upon. "Want some tea?"

"Yes, please."

I sink into one of the chairs at the counter.

What an imagination I've got going tonight. I'm hallucinating the ghost of Adam warning me to get the hell out of Mandy's house. But Mandy's been nothing but nice to me since I've arrived. She's great. There can't be even a speck of evil in that adorable little body of hers.

Once the water boils, Mandy takes out two mugs and fixes our drinks. She sets my tea in front of me and I immediately start drinking. It's hot, but if I blow a little cool air it makes the heat less intense against my lips.

"Mmm," I say. "This is good. What kind is it?"

Mandy adds a squeeze of blue agave from a bottle into her tea, then stirs it in with a spoon. "Honey lavender. It helps with stress."

"It's got something else in here I like."

"So your flight's at eleven tomorrow?"

"Uh huh."

Mandy takes a sip from her mug. "Does your brother or anybody even know you're in Pasadena?"

"Kyle knows I'm out. We have a rule now. We tell each other exactly where we are right before we go to bed. After what happened to Adam it's... it's for the best. He's going to be so pissed I'm all the way out in Pasadena."

I chuckle about this and rest my hand against my forehead, envisioning his reaction when I call him later to check-in. I take a final swig of the tea and set the mug down.

Mandy acknowledges the empty cup and takes both mugs over to the sink.

"I'm heading back to bed," she says. "You coming?"

"In a minute. Thanks again. For the tea. For the ride tomorrow. You're really great, Mandy."

Mandy breaks into a smile. "Only because you are."

Once Mandy's upstairs, I head over to the closet to retrieve my phone from my jacket pocket. Just like my jeans, the phone is nowhere to be found. I sigh. Did I take it with me into the bedroom? Is it on the nightstand in Mandy's room or something?

I open my mouth to say something, but I stop myself. What if Mandy's the one who took it? Would she really do something like that?

I shut the closet door and I'm about to head upstairs when I catch a glimpse of the closet by the front door. The one she told me to stay out of earlier tonight.

Weird Totally-Not-Real Doll Adam, I don't know what it is you're expecting me to find here...

I tread slowly across the creaky floor and open the closet door, expecting something to fall off the shelf since Mandy claimed it was a mess. But the only thing in the closet is a box on the ground. I kneel down and remove the lid from the top of the box. It looks like a bunch of random stuff...

Until I find Adam's jacket. The dark blue one he was wearing the night he left.

Followed by his wallet. His ID, money, credit cards. They're all still in here.

Brooks' wallet is in here, too.

And a pair of sunglasses with his name engraved on the inside of the right temple.

There's also a cracked phone that I recognize as Adam's. It has the same silver case that he had right before he disappeared. I also find what appears to be a leasing contract for Mandy's house. I scan through the document...

WTF...?

Mandy's renting from Charlie Monroe! I slide Adam's phone into my pocket as evidence... or something... I don't even know at this point. All I know is Mandy's a psychopath.

Sure, I could try to convince myself that she just stole this stuff. That she somehow managed to get a hold of the wallets and cell phones. Possibly bought them off eBay by some sick jerk. But no. I can't risk that. I'm in danger the longer I stay here.

I grab my jacket from the closet and slide it on. It doesn't even matter that I don't have shoes on. I'll manage until I can get the hell out of here. Mandy can even keep my phone for all I care. It's password protected and I can have it shut off tomorrow.

But there *is* something I need...

"Adam?" I whisper out loud. I wander around downstairs, hoping to find that damn doll. I have to take it. What if Adam is still capable of being saved?

"Adam?" I repeat. "I believe you now. I'm leaving, but I'm taking you with me. Where are you? Adam? Adam?"

But that's when the drowsiness kicks in. I stumble forward, feeling the world sway and spin. I shake my head, but it makes me even dizzier. I close my eyes. I *have* to find Adam and get out of here. I can get through this…

All it takes is one more step forward, and everything goes black.

⁂

I open my eyes.

I'm in a dark room and I'm seated in an old, wooden chair.

Actually, scratch that.

I'm *tied up* in an old, wooden chair. There are candles lit all around me on the ground, along with white and red flower pedals. Am I about to be sacrificed?

There's a washer machine and dryer to my left, and a stairway to my right. I'm in the basement. Funny how we skipped *this* room on her little tour.

How am I supposed to get out of here?

My only hope at this point would be Adam. Where is he?

"Looking for this?" Mandy says, holding up Doll Adam.

"Let him go."

"Please, Rick. Do you think I'm stupid?"

Mandy opens a mini safe sitting on the dryer and tosses Doll Adam inside of it. Then she slams the safe shut and locks it. She's got her back to me so I can't see the combination.

"He won't be going anywhere. And neither will you."

Mandy circles around my chair. Every now and again she'll run her fingers through my hair or let her fingertips sweep against my shoulders.

"You see, I am a collector, Rick. I used to collect limited edition posters. Concert ticket stubs. Whatever I could find online that seemed valuable. But that wasn't what I wanted. I didn't desire the memorabilia. I wanted *real*. More one of a kind than one of a kind. What's more one of a kind than the actual thing?"

"You're a monster."

"I'm no monster, Rick. I love my dolls with all my heart. They mean everything to me. I did take your brother. And I love him. So much. Were you going to take him away from me?"

"Mandy, please…"

Mandy wraps her arms around me and kisses my temple. "Don't worry. You'll get to be with your brother. And Kyle will be reunited with you soon."

What's she talking about?

Mandy must notice I'm suspicious, because she pulls my phone out from her back jean pocket and holds it up. She types in a code and reads my most recent text message. "Looks like he's on his way."

"Stop texting my brother!"

She just laughs as she texts.

"What do you want, Mandy? I'll give you whatever you want."

"Don't be silly, Rick. I want you."

Mandy reaches for something on a tall shelf.

"Oh, no…" I moan. Because I know exactly what she's cradling in her arms.

A doll.

Mandy steps in front of me and I'm face to face with the doll that will become me. Or, I will become *it*. I have no idea how this works. How am I going to end up in that *thing*?

Mandy holds up a brown leather book that looks a thousand years old. Some of the aged pages are loose and ready to fall out.

I can't let Mandy do this to me. I have to get out of here.

I do a quick sweep around the room to try to find *something*. Anything. You've got to have something here for me, Mandy. That's when I figure it out.

"Can you please let me be with Adam when it happens? Please, Mandy? I want him to be here when it happens."

Mandy raises a single eyebrow, then glances over at the safe.

"Fine," she says, and walks across the room.

I stand up as much as I can with my hands tied and sprint toward Mandy. She doesn't even see me coming when

I shove her against the wall with all my strength. This causes her to bang her head against the wall and she falls to the ground.

"God, please forgive me for hurting a girl."

I go over to a table full of tools and search the sharpest thing that I can find (a pocket knife!), cut the rope, and untie myself. When I'm finally free, I head over to the safe and try to figure out the combo.

"What is it, Adam?"

Try something harder than your brother's birthdate.

I shrug and take a guess. Might as well.

I try nine-one-four. For September fourteenth. Adam's birthday.

The safe opens and I grab Adam.

Now it's time to get out of here. I turn around to head up the stairs when I feel a sharp pain in my left calf. I pause and scream, then I look down. Mandy stabbed me with that damn pocket knife.

"I have a show tomorrow, you bitch!" I shriek.

That's it. No more playing nice. I kick Mandy's hand and the knife goes flying onto the floor feet away from her. Despite all the blood on her face that's dripping down her forehead and running along the side of her temple, she manages to crawl toward the knife pretty quickly.

I yank the fire extinguisher off the wall and spray it at

Mandy. While Mandy's struggling to see, I grab a plastic gasoline can and spill as much gasoline as I can on the ground around Mandy and me. I try to get the bottom of the stairs too. I kick the knife a little further so she has to go out of her way to retrieve it, then I kick over all the candles until a fire starts. I grab one candle and that book.

"No!" Mandy yells, still on her knees with her face covered in dry powder from the fire extinguisher and her own blood. "Don't leave me down here, Rick! Please!"

"Sorry, Mandy. Turns out this isn't what I'm used to. Pasadena's not really for me."

I throw the candle at the foot of the stairs and the fire spreads. The floor is barely visible anymore.

I dart upstairs, then shut the door and lock it as Mandy's screams fill my ears. I press my back to the door and sigh.

I glance at Doll Adam.

We're safe, bro.

I try to drown out the sounds of Mandy hopefully burning alive as I set Doll Adam on the kitchen counter and open up the book. I go through the index until I find what I assume is the reversal spell for transforming people into inanimate objects.

I repeat the chant out loud, three times like it says, and a cloud of black smoke rises from the floor. It travels to the ceiling, and while I do smell the fire downstairs, I know that this smoke is coming from something else entirely.

The smoke forms around the doll, and when the smoke starts to vanish, a human body is in the place where the doll once laid. It's Adam. Dressed in the same white T-shirt and blue pants with white sneakers he was wearing the night he disappeared.

Adam lifts his head, then sits up and pats his hands against random spots on his body like he's trying to figure out if he's still a doll or not. Then he looks up at me.

"Am I...?" he starts.

I nod, a big smile on my face.

"Dude," Adam says, and we embrace.

The doorbell rings and we both head over the front door to answer it.

"Hey..." Kyle says. He pops his head in to get a look around, then when his eyes fall on Adam, they widen in disbelief.

"It's really me," Adam says.

Kyle laughs and hugs Adam. As much as I'm loving this reunion, there's an insane person down in the basement who may be dead, but may not be.

"We need to get out of here," I say, grabbing onto Kyle's shoulders to guide him out. "Like... *now*."

Kyle takes one last glance around as we head out the door. "Who's place is this anyway?"

NINA – A Few Years Later

"Mommy, I want this one," my daughter Kitty says. She's eyeing a doll on a rack full of them at Toys 'R Fun. We've been here for ten minutes searching for something for her to splurge her birthday money on. I'm relieved she's finally found *something* she's interested in.

I kneel down to get a good look at the doll. It looks so unlike all the other dolls. She's got oversized, animated green eyes and firey red hair. The hair even feels real to the touch.

"She's cute," I say, and hand the doll back to her.

"Do you think Daddy would mind? You know he hates dolls."

I pat Kitty on the head. "I think Daddy would make an exception for her."

Kitty goes back to admiring the doll when a woman approaches us. "I'm *so* sorry to bother you," the woman whispers. "But are you Nina Jerry? *Rick* Jerry's wife?"

I look down, embarrassed. Well, not actually. It's just become a force of habit. That's what happens when you marry a celebrity. Especially someone as big as Rick. You're famous by association. "That would be me," I say politely.

"Could I get a picture?" the fan holds up her phone.

I nod and grab her shoulder to get close to her so she can

take our selfie.

"Mommy, can we get her, please?" Kitty begs.

"Yeah, let's ring her up," I say, then turn to the woman. "We have to go. It was good to meet you, though."

Kitty and I head over to the register hand in hand. Kitty turns the doll upside down and tries to read something written on the bottom of her shoe. "The doll has a name, Mom!"

"Oh, what is it?" I say, but I'm only half paying attention as I pull out my wallet. We're next in line and I like to be ready.

"Mandy," she says, and repeats it again like it's the most perfect name for a doll.

"Your dad's going to hate that name." The cashier returns my credit card to me and hands me the receipt.

Kitty holds up the doll and smiles at her. "I can't wait for you to meet my dad," she whispers, and we head home.

THE RAVINE

BY MALCOLM BADEWITZ

THE HOUSE SAT alone. Its porch sagged. Nettles wrestled for control of the pale yard. And every night, as the sun retreated behind the trees, a boy threw open the back door, leapt over the porch, and bounded across the tangled weeds.

His sneakers kicked dust from the uneven earth, dodging the molehills and ivy reaching to trip him. He noted every perilous irregularity, and as the yard sloped down, the boy shifted his weight back so as not to tumble forward. The reeds towered overhead, then opened impossibly on both sides, giving way to the mouth of the great ravine. The boy's footsteps softened. He slowed to catch his breath, and tip-toed to the ledge...

He peered down through the bottomless patchwork of sticker bushes, and was sure it was there -- a fearsome thing, gazing up through the dark. Squaring off with him.

The boy's mother called from the house.

But he did not answer.

He needed to focus. To remember every groove, every molehill, and pitfall. It would mean life or death, he knew, when on some summer night, while his parents slept, long fingers of ivy would creep up the embankment, and across the lawn. To twist through his window, to snatch him up, and drag him back through the night, through the pale yard, to the rotting mouth of the ravine. But he'd be prepared. He'd know every groove, molehill, and pitfall. He'd know the land better than the land itself.

His mother called again.

The boy peered down through the rotting foliage. And just before the sun disappeared behind the trees, he darted back to the house.

But the changing seasons brought new things for the boy to explore, beyond the backyard. In the fall, his mother took him to school, and in the summer, to play with the boys he'd met there. Every year his life filled with exciting, wonderful successes, failures, people and places, and so went the ravine, and the fearful thing inside.

The house stands today. No one has come to water the yard, nor disrupt its weeds. His mother no longer lives here, but the boy has come to remember her. As he rounds the house, the yellow grass beneath his feet feels just as it did back then. The porch sags just as it did when his mother used to stand on it, calling out to him. He remembers the frustration in her voice. He remembers his nightly ritual.

Sun-baked nettles still wrestle for the yard. The uneven earth still kicks dust as he walks. He remembers how perilous it seemed -- the molehills, divots, and nettle patches. His strides are longer now. He makes quick work of them. But he still slows at the thought of twisting an ankle.

The soil grows soft underfoot. The reeds cast thin shadows as he approaches the mouth of the ravine. He remembers the trick of shifting his weight so as not to tumble. He remembers how he came to know that trick. He remembers the fearful thing.

He peers down through the rotting foliage.

Silent.

Listening.

And in his mind's eye, he sees it looking back up at him, sizing him up for the first time in years. Surely it sees that he is taller now, his clothes plain, his face long and worn. A grown-up, not to be startled by imaginary things.

The man lifts his head. He glances at the sun retreating behind the pines, and just before it disappears, he darts back to his car.

Scab

BY DANIEL LEE

ON MY FIRST day, I walked past the picket line to the loading dock behind the grocery store, where a manager ushered a group of us quickly through the back door. We were issued aprons without nametags and given assignments. All day long I worked the register, watching customers walk sideways between picketers to buy milk and Jimmy Deans, and every time the automatic doors slid open, my eyes met those of the union workers outside, who stared me down in anger. I'd look away, anxiously scratching my head as I greeted the next customer. By the end of the day my hair resembled the splayed bristles of a worn-out toothbrush.

On my second day, picketers had blocked the back entrance, so we had to wait for the police to remove them before we could get inside. Had I known that on this day I'd be stocking dairy products, I'd have brought a coat and gloves. As it was, I spent the day freezing so that my numb fingertips couldn't feel my itchy scalp as I scratched. By the time I got home I still hadn't fully regained sensation, and hardly registered my sleeping nine-year-old daughter Penny's soft cheek as I caressed it. Through the cardboard taped over the broken window of our fourth-story apartment, a man and woman could be heard arguing relentlessly in the alley outside. I sat on the couch examining the three-day notice to pay or quit that I had found taped to our door as the TV news spoke of the president inciting potential civil war.

I picked at my head. Everything would be fine.

On day three, I was back at the register until a picketer rushed inside and began knocking wine bottles off the shelves, at which point I was tasked with mopping up the floor, sticky with vermilion shards of glass. For several moments the sight reminded me of the pavement where Mira had landed, of shielding Penny's eyes, and I stood with a mop in one hand, the fingers of the other probing my sore scalp. My nail found the lip of a healing wound and, without thinking, peeled it away, exposing a fresh divot underneath. Upon inspection, I found I'd torn off a small flake of dry skin with a red center like a demonic eye. The manager called me back to attention, so I flicked the flake to the floor and proceeded to clean up the spilled wine.

Day four. Apparently corporate had held a pow-wow with union reps to lay out a possible compromise, to no avail, so work continued. I spent fifteen minutes helping a customer find a jar of sun butter, which I later found discarded among the cleaning products. Another customer asked to return a half-eaten jar of pickles because they weren't kosher. An itch on my head attracted my fingers, which detected a crystalline stalagmite congealed on my scalp. I found an odd pleasure in the feel of it, but inadvertently scooped it away with my ring finger. Caked beneath my nail was a gummy red wedge that I rolled onto my fingertip with my thumbnail and pinched into two segments before casting it to the void as a customer approached asking for a refund on eggs she'd purchased and immediately dropped on the way to her car.

On day five of the strike, I surreptitiously approached one of the protesters outside to ask about joining the union. "Screw you," he responded. That's when I was spotted by the manager and told to collect my things and get out of his store. Despite my begging he sent me on my way. I picked at my head the entire bus ride home, sifting between hair follicles for previously tilled earth, continuing my excavations as I stared unblinkingly out the window at tents and makeshift camps pitched every few yards along the sidewalk. I imagined living like that with my daughter, and again ripped a crust from my scalp, wincing as I looked down to find my finger covered in blood.

Everything would be fine.

I picked up my pay on day six, averting my eyes from the death stares of both the strikers and the breakers, pressing my fingertips to my head as I crossed the line. I gnashed my teeth as I waited in the bank queue to deposit my check. Saw a couple speaking with a banker. Arguing, crying, splitting their savings. And I remembered sitting in those same seats with Mira two months earlier. Found another calcified formation on my scalp and plucked it out, felt a sting and the cool breath of open air on the wound as though I'd popped a cork. Approached the teller at the call of "Next?" and listened as she explained politely that I was overdrawn, that the bank procedure required intercepting my deposit for the payment of penalty fees.

Time stopped then as the world spun about me. I saw my daughter living in a tent on the sidewalk, the sneering of protesters picketing nearby, the barking of a grocery store manager, the complaining of customers, my divorce from Mira, her leap from our apartment window, the pavement where she'd landed, smashed wine bottles, shards of red glass.

"Sir?" came a panicked voice from behind me. "Your head!"

"My... head?" I lowered my fingers to find my hand drenched in blood.

"Mister, I can see your skull!"

My wet digits shot back to my head, where in my horror

I'd torn open my scalp and proceeded to scratch at the hard bone beneath. I could feel it smooth to the touch and pocked with craters worn thin from years of digging. My finger slid inside one and began to scrape.

"No, sir! Stop!"

Gasps and screams rose around me but I couldn't stop. I scraped and chiseled and picked and probed until I was numb with pleasure and compelled still to continue. My face twitched involuntarily, my free arm flailed, my body convulsed. My finger withdrew, and with it came slippery ropes of lobster meat that fell with gloppy splats to the floor.

I noticed then the people around me smiling. I saw the teller turn her computer screen to me, revealing my account balance. She laughed. It had all been a joke. I had more than enough. I saw the bank doors open, saw Penny run through them to embrace me, Mira at her side.

Everything was fine. We'd be just fine.

How Do You Kill A Dead Cat?

by Sean Cameron

"*I HAVE ONE* hard rule… I can't bring back the dead." Sydney slurped her beer.

"So, you tried?"

As she leaned closer, the tips of her blonde hair brushed along her shoulders. "I don't like to talk about it."

Andrew pushed his pint to the side so he could lean across the table. "So you can?"

Sydney paused. She eyed the dimly lit pub. The velvet chairs surrounding the mismatched tables were all empty. It was a typically quiet Tuesday afternoon. The distant barman played with his phone with little care for his surroundings.

She narrowed her eyes. "Fine, I have one rule, I *won't* bring back the dead."

Andrew flashed a smile, showing off his perfect teeth. "You got me all intrigued now. What did you do?"

Sydney sat back. The pair were too close for her liking.

"Are you serious about hiring me?"

"Of course."

"Because you're acting like we're on a date." Sydney swallowed her beer with a wince. She wasn't used to the taste, but felt she had to drink now that she was old enough.

Andrew ignored her response. "You still speak to spirits? Not like a Ouija board, I mean straight-up seeing and hearing a spirit."

"I've spoken with spirits, but only I can see and hear them."

"And who'd you bring back from the dead?"

"We don't talk about that."

"Come on."

Sydney played with her bottle, twisting it clockwise on the dog-eared beer mat. "How's college going?"

Andrew raised his eyebrows. "I thought this wasn't a date?"

"Small talk is still permitted."

Andrew laughed. "It was... fine."

"That all?"

"I got through my first year, not much else to report. I've been home for a couple of weeks, and I spoke to someone that might need your services."

"Which of my services?"

Andrew hesitated. "I... I want some information... from

a ghost."

Sydney didn't flinch. "Spirit. Why?"

"I need a straight answer."

"I know how you feel."

Andrew rolled his bright blue eyes. "You're standoffish, you know that?"

Sydney huffed. "I noticed you at my grandmother's funeral you know. It was autumn, so you'd started uni."

"I was in town visiting my parents."

"You sat in the back row."

"Was that weird?"

"I know you two liked each other. It's kind of sweet you came, but you avoided me. Now, you text me to ask if I still do 'the pentagram thing.' And you casually tell me you want me to summon a spirit. Excuse me for being a little standoffish."

Andrew grinned. "I accept your apology."

"I wasn't–"

"You wanna know who you're gonna commune with?"

"Yes."

"Did you ever meet Leah McGuire? She was in the year above me. Her cousin Tommy was quiet. He always focused on his schoolwork. Then came his last year at school, he worried he'd been missing out. So he decided to try out the under-eighteen night at The Monte Carlo."

"I hate that place."

"It's totally dead now. Literally… I mean, not literally dead in the sense you'd mean. I mean dead like how everyone else means. Quiet. But this was six months ago. Tommy, he tried messaging his classmates to see if they wanted to come, but no one was interested. He went anyway, hoping to see some familiar faces. He put on a nice shirt, put some product in his hair, and headed down to the club. After ordering a lemonade, he looked around and he saw the friends that he texted."

"The ones that didn't want to go?"

"Yeah, they were already there."

"Ouch."

"Tommy got upset and stormed out. He messaged Leah, she's kind of a big sister to him."

"And?"

"Her phone was on silent so she missed the text. Tommy goes missing. A couple of days later, his body was found in the river. The bridge was part of his walk home, but he didn't make it to the other side."

Sydney furrowed her brow. "He killed himself over that?"

"That's what's eating Leah. Did he kill himself? Could she have saved him if she replied in time?"

"What else could have happened?"

"Tommy had a bully or two. As he ran out, he accidentally shoved one of them."

"And that'll warrant being murdered?"

Andrew shrugged, "Maybe a fight that went too far."

"So, Leah wants some peace of mind from her cousin?"

"Exactly."

"She's not trying to bring him back or anything? She knows that's off the table."

Andrew raised his palms. "A simple Q&A."

"Sorry, people always ask. They always want to bring someone back."

"What happened?"

Sydney's shoulders dropped. "A cat. A girl wanted her cat back. It was a recent death, so it seemed possible."

"But?"

She winced. "You can bring the spirit back to the cat's body, but that doesn't make the body alive. It hissed and scratched and constantly meowed, like a scream. It was very upset."

"Wow, did you undo it?"

"The incantations aren't in English so I didn't know how. I only have my grandmother's notes telling me what they do."

"Did you kill it?"

"How do you kill a dead cat? You just make it angrier."

"So, what happened?"

"We caught it." She let out a deep breath. "And buried

it. Deep."

Andrew tucked in his chin. He put his hands on the table, then his lap. He no longer knew how to sit comfortably. "That's... horrible."

"I'm not proud. Tell Leah I can meet with her tomorrow evening at Eggland."

"Eggland? Where's that?"

"I'll send you the address. We'll need a couple of Tommy's personal items and an animal sacrifice."

"An animal sacrifice? I thought it would just be--"

"This isn't a Ouija board. We're dealing with real dark magic. There's a cost. There's always a cost."

"But an animal sacrifice?"

"Nothing too big. A mouse is fine."

"What about a cricket?"

"A mouse is fine."

Sydney stood outside the white stone church. It was tall with a short steeple. She pushed through the cut chain-link fence and smiled at a sign. It read 'The C urch O E gland;" the reason she'd affectionately renamed the building *Eggland*. She stroked the bottom edge of the cracked wooden sign as she walked by, a ritual of hers.

An unkempt garden surrounded the church. Sydney walked around to the side unseen by traffic. Overgrown weeds shot from the cracks in the pavement. Around the corner, Andrew waited with Leah. She had long red hair and wore a flowery dress. Leah's eyes were glassy like she might cry at any second.

"I'm Sydney."

"Hi... Leah." She put on a smile.

Sydney turned to Andrew. "Did you bring the offering?"

He held up a small thin box with holes. "Mouse from the pet store."

Leah's eyes darted between the pair. "What's that for?"

Sydney kept walking. "It's best not to think about it."

She passed the decorative wooden double doors and climbed a storage box to reach a boarded-up window. Sydney pulled the corner, and the wood board fell. The window had a whole panel missing, large enough to crawl through.

Sydney climbed onto the stone sill and slid her legs in first. "There's a stepladder on the other side, just lower yourself slowly until your feet find it."

She dropped into the darkness. Andrew followed and led Leah down.

A dim light from the highest windows lit the interior, highlighting the dusty air. It took a moment for their eyes to adjust to the darkness. The walls were the same white stone as outside, with a blacked-out corner from a long-ago fire. The pews had been pushed to the side which created space for a red-painted pentagram on the wood floor. Sydney lit the candles that circled the pentagram.

Leah swallowed. "Is this going to be OK?"

Andrew put his hand on her back to comfort her. "It's fine."

"Depends who you ask," Sydney said as she lit the last candle. "It's messing with the dark arts, but we're not hurting anyone."

"Except the mouse," Andrew said.

Leah recoiled.

"OK, the mouse gets hurt. But it was snake food anyway. Its days were numbered."

"And Tommy?" Leah asked.

"Your cousin doesn't have to accept the invitation. No harm can come to him." Sydney sat cross-legged in the pentagram. "Did you bring the items?"

Andrew nodded. He opened his bag and placed a locket and a comb in the centre of the pentagram.

Sydney leaned into Andrew's ear. "These are her cousin's things?"

"That's what she said." He seemed nervous.

Sydney gave Andrew an assuring smile. "You OK to do this?"

"Of course," he stuttered. He opened the box and held the mouse as it sniffed Andrew's fingers.

After a deep breath, Sydney glanced at Leah. "Step towards the candles and wait there. Don't speak until I have invited you. It will be after your cousin's spirit is here. I will speak for him. Don't be alarmed."

After taking a deep breath, Sydney took her grandmother's notebook from her coat pocket. She spoke the ancient words, not understanding the meaning, but knowing the end result. Wind blew from the altar, pushing the candles' flames. Instead of blowing them out, they burnt brighter.

As Sydney read the next passage, a calm cyclone of dust blew around them.

She raised her hands and said the rest. She nodded at Andrew; he winced as he squeezed the mouse's neck. The little critter squealed and flung its short legs until its neck snapped. Andrew threw it down into the pentagram.

A flash of light followed by a pulse knocked the three back. The pews rumbled and dragged back. Sydney had never seen that happen before.

A growing light shone from the centre of the pentagram. Sydney rushed to her feet.

Leah stepped back from the painted edge. "Is this normal?"

Andrew beckoned Leah back into her position. She

shook her head in a short, sharp manner.

The light, almost a spotlight from nowhere, flickered brightly. Her eyes stinging, Sydney looked away and saw Andrew squinting. He wasn't supposed to see anything. Something was wrong.

The light dimmed into a grey, hunched over figure. Its head was gaunt with straw-like white hair. The eyes were more like black holes. It's white gown faded as it met the ground.

"Are you the spirit of Tommy?" Sydney asked.

The figure studied Andrew, Sydney, and Leah. It did not speak.

"What is that?" Leah asked.

Sydney darted a look at the terrified girl.

The figure pushed forward, passing Sydney and leaving the pentagram.

Sydney swallowed. "Uh, it's not meant to be able to do that."

The figure beelined towards Leah. She screamed and ran, tripping on a metal bucket half-filled with collected rainwater. A puddle poured across the wood floor.

Sydney scanned through the notebook, looking at her grandmother's notes. There had to be something to repel this creature. She looked at Andrew. He stood back in frozen panic.

The figure's hands reached out for Leah, its digits were thin and long. Leah raced to the church's reception as it darted after her.

Sydney reached a page in the notebook. The notes said, 'incantation to ward off evil spirits.' She read the first few sentences.

The figure stopped its pursuit and spun towards Sydney, who continued to read. It screamed and a force blew the book from Sydney's hands, sliding her notes across the floor.

Andrew ran. "I'll get it." He grabbed the book and dashed back, but tripped and dropped it at the pentagram's edge. He reached for the notebook but knocked over a candle, lighting a corner of the book. In a panic, he tried to slap the flame out but hurt his hand.

Sydney rushed to the book and stamped out the flames.

The figure reached for Leah, its hand passing through her chest. Leah screamed and passed out. She fell, cracking her head on the corner of a stone wall. As her head landed on the ground, a pool of blood grew.

Sydney's stomach sank as she saw Leah's body. She opened the notebook to the spell, but the top half of the page had blackened.

The figure glided towards the pair.

Andrew stepped back. "Uh, do you have any ideas?"

Sydney took a deep breath. "This isn't like a normal

spirit, it's not supposed to be here. It's supposed to be more like, I don't know, a video chat. This thing managed to get through."

Although the figure's feet were unseen, the dust on the ground shifted leaving footprints.

Sydney grabbed the locket and comb from the pentagram. "These things brought it here, but how? She opened the locket and saw a young couple, a man on one side, a woman on the other. She recognised the girl. She knew the eyes and the smile. It was her grandmother, and the boy was her grandfather.

"Those are my grandparents." She turned to Andrew. "Why did Leah have a locket of my grandparents?"

Andrew grabbed Sydney's shoulders. "Are you sure?"

"Yes, I know my grandparents when I see them."

Andrew pulled Sydney to the right, squeezing her shoulders tight.

"What are you doing?" she said.

Sydney turned behind her and saw the figure approach. It's pointy fingers reaching out. Its mouth stretched open.

"Let go of me."

"I'm sorry, Deary," Andrew said.

"Deary?"

"It's the only way."

Sydney kicked at Andrew as he grasped her coat sleeve.

There was no way she was going to be his human shield. She kicked harder. He fell back and let go.

Sydney bent back to avoid the figure's hand. Although it hadn't touched her, she felt a sharp cold sensation from being so close. The shock of it emptied Sydney's lungs. She jumped back and Andrew grabbed her foot. Sydney shook his grip loose and stomped on his hand.

She raced for the window they'd all climbed down. The figure screamed with a force of wind that knocked over the stepladder. Sydney tried to pick it back up, but the figure glided too fast. Backing away, Sydney ran towards the steps into the reception area. She shoved the double doors, but they wouldn't budge.

The figure floated over the steps leading into the reception. Sydney was trapped. She sidestepped away from the door and ran into the women's toilet.

Only a little light made it into the room from a high up window with cracked glass. She stepped on the toilet seat to open the window. The handle broke off in her grip. She cried tears of desperation, but no sound came from her mouth.

The figure glided through the doorway over cracked tiles. A sink half dangled above a dirty mirror.

"What do you want?" Sydney screamed.

As the figure passed into the light from the window, Sydney saw its reflection in the mirror. Behind the scratched and dirty marks of the mirror she saw her grandmother seemingly alive and well. The reflection faded as the figure left the spotlight.

"Nana?"

The figure paused.

"What's happening? Why are you here?"

The figure pointed at her.

Andrew walked through the doorway.

"Andrew, I thought you ran away."

He stepped in the spotlight with a smile. "You don't get it. Do you, Deary?" He nodded to the mirror.

Sydney saw Andrew's reflection. It wasn't the young boy she knew, but an old man. Her grandfather. Sydney shuffled back until she bumped into the wall. She raced into the cubicle and came out holding a cistern lid high.

Andrew tsked. "You can't fight her. You can't stop her. She's not alive."

"I'm not aiming for her."

Sydney threw the cistern lid. It passed through the figure and into Andrew, the porcelain clonked against his raised arms, knocking him to the ground. The cistern landed on his left side. He screamed.

Sydney raced out the door to the altar, far away from the pair. As she passed the pentagram she grabbed her notebook.

The figure and a limping Andrew followed her towards the altar.

"How long has Andrew been gone?" Sydney screamed. "How long?"

"About a year," Andrew said.

"So, right when we broke up?"

"Essentially."

"It was you that attended her funeral."

"Yes."

"Nana did this for you, didn't she? Gave you Andrew's body."

"And now you have raised her, and must give her your body."

"Or what?"

"Or we shall take it."

The figure raised a palm at heart level. Sydney felt the cold grow in her chest as the figure glided closer.

"No, I'll fight you." She turned the notebook pages, scanning for something to help.

The figure and Andrew stepped closer. "Nothing in there will stop us."

"You wanted to use me to take over Leah?"

"It's unfortunate that it worked out this way."

The figure's gaunt face winced.

Sydney sighed. "What will happen to me?"

"Your life will end." Andrew peered down. "It's not so bad."

"Not good enough to stay dead though, right?"

Sydney flicked through the pages of her burnt book. Behind the figure laid the body of Leah. Sydney stopped on the spell that brought back the dead cat. She could trap her grandmother in the corpse of Leah. Forever stuck in pain and struggle.

Sydney said the words on the page. Not able to understand them, just knowing it worked before.

The figure seized up.

"What's happening?" Andrew asked.

Sydney continued with the spell. The figure faded, drawn to Leah's body.

Andrew ran, snatched the book from Sydney, and tossed it across the room. It was just a chant at this point, easily repeated.

The figure appeared more opaque than before, weak and unable to move. Andrew grabbed Sydney and pulled her to the figure. Her grandmother reached out its hand. Sydney's chest hurt again. She couldn't move, but she wouldn't be silenced. She continued the chant. The figure snarled.

Sydney's chest pounded with overwhelming pain until it suddenly went numb. She faded into darkness. Unable to move her lips, Sydney repeated the chant in her head, at least she thought she was still in her head. She thought about Leah's body and how she could possess Leah. She could at least attack her grandparents before they left the church. She thought the chant until the words quietened into nothing.

The pain returned. Instead of coldness, it felt like thousands of pinpricks over her body, a body that wasn't hers. Had she done it? A living spirit trapped in the dead body of Leah? She tried to move her limbs, but they didn't feel right. Every movement was excruciating. Her vision was blurry but gained focus. Her first instinct was to gasp for air, but a dead body doesn't need oxygen. Her eyes focused. Everything seemed so much larger.

She saw Andrew help up her grandmother, now possessing Sydney's body. They embraced in a loving hug. Behind them lay the corpse of Leah. How could she see Leah? Sydney realised what had happened. She was in the dead mouse. Trapped in a rodent. Unable to leave it. Unable to end the phantom pains.

She watched Andrew put the ladder back so the pair could climb out.

Sydney shuffled her feet and took her first steps. Although each move hurt, she crawled along the floor and squeezed under the double doors.

Not much could be done as a mouse, but she could bide

her time. At the perfect moment, she could startle them while driving or cooking; something that could cause a life-threatening mistake. Failing that, she could torment them all their days. What could they do?

After all, how do you kill a dead mouse?

Hanging Out With Hannah's Friends

by Ben Greene

I HAD ONLY been dating Hannah for three months, but things felt like they were going really well. We were always totally in sync about where to go to dinner or what we wanted to watch on Netflix. We even had the same favorite *The Spiral Dragons* song!

There was a time with my last girlfriend, Anna, where I threw a hand full of sand at her while we were on the beach as a joke (I can't really remember what the exact joke was, but it felt like a fun thing to do in the moment) and she got so angry at me, it ended up being a huge fight.

Well, Hannah is completely different. I mean, their names are even different: Hannah and Anna, totally dissimilar. Hannah is the kind of girl who will laugh really hard when I do something like that and throw a bunch of sand right back at me. More than anything she's just really easy going, and after three months of dating I was starting to think about how fun it would be if our relationship lasted a while.

It was a couple weeks into November when Hannah mentioned that her friends were going to be going to this haunted house kind of thing down by the old fairground. I thought it was kind of weird that something Halloween-ish was still happening well after Halloween itself, and to be honest, I don't really like that kind of thing, but Hannah had mentioned that she really wanted me to spend more time with her group of friends. So in the end I said I would go.

As we walked to the haunted house, I pulled the sleeves of my jacket over my hands. It was way colder than I thought it was going to be, just getting into hurt-your-face territory. It was me, Hannah's friend Brett, her childhood best friend Sarah, and Sarah's friend Amy who was weirdly wearing an outfit almost exactly the same as Hannah, same red shirt and Old Navy jeans.

As we got closer, I talked to Brett, who I had only met once before. I knew that Brett and Hannah had dated very briefly in high school, but when I joked months ago about being threatened by him, Hannah laughed really hard and told me that he was way too dumb to ever be a long term boyfriend. He used to lie about books he had read, saying he had read them when he had actually only seen the movie.

While we walked toward the haunted house Brett tried

to get in my head about the experience. "This isn't like one of those rides in Disneyland where you're in a little seat and all the ghosts are singing. Things get pretty freaky in here. They're allowed to touch you and push your limits as much as they want."

"I mean, not as much as they want," I said. "They wouldn't do anything that would, like, make someone sue them."

"You can't sue them! Everyone signs a thing before they go in that basically says you can't sue them for anything, even if you somehow got like, badly hurt in there."

Sarah chimed in and noted that they still had a policy where if you yell, "I WANT TO GET OUT!" they have to let you out.

"Yeah," said Brett, "And then everyone knows what a lame-o you are. You're like that guy who abandons the kids in Jurassic Park, the *book* by Michael Whatever-his-name-is."

I rolled my eyes.

When we finally got to the haunted house we all signed our release forms and went in. The first room looked like a very realistic portrayal of a meth head's living room, with fake drugs all over the floor and fake broken glass and a broken TV. It was weirdly hot in there, like sauna hot, though there was no steam. It felt weird for it to be that hot when we were only one door away from the outside, and it also struck me that it was strange that no one had warned us about the heat. I took off my jacket and tried to toss it outside, but the door wouldn't open. So I just tied my jacket around my waist and walked onwards, feeling very hot. I found myself looking at a broken picture on the wall, a posed graduation picture of a high school girl.

POUND, POUND, POUND!!!

I stumbled back, someone had pounded on the wall behind the picture, and it scared the heck-a-roonie out of me. Then there was more pounding, but now it was happening in every corner of the room.

'How do they do that?' I wondered. It's a pretty good effect. I moved close to Hannah. I could tell she didn't want to be too close because of the heat, but she'd also promised me that she'd stay close by. She knew this kind of thing wasn't my favorite.

We moved on into a long dark hallway. It seemed to go on for a really long time. I tried to figure out the geography of the house we were in, it didn't seem like it was that big when we were outside, but this hallway was massive. Maybe it was a trick with mirrors? But how would that work?

I felt a presence behind me and turned around, but I didn't see anything. Then, a horrible scream filled the hallway. It was awful. I tried covering my ears to block it out, but it was so loud that even with my ears covered it was still piercing. Then something grabbed my leg and pulled it hard, so I fell right over. I fell on my back and felt the pain ringing through it immediately. My hands had left my ears for the moment, and now the screaming wasn't blocked out at all. It surrounded me and my heart felt cold. Because I was having absolutely no fun at all, I thought about calling "I want to get out" at that moment, but I knew how embarrassing it would be to flake out and have to wait for Hannah's friends outside.

Instead, as the screaming died down, I tried to amp myself up and get in the mood of the haunted house. I thought I might have some fun and be a little playful and try to scare Hannah, so I went up to her and grabbed her butt. She jumped around and looked horrified. It wasn't Hannah; it was Amy in those stupid Old Navy jeans. She yelled at me, "What the hell are you doing?" and I saw Hannah looking at me disgusted. I tried to explain myself but then the scream came back and the lights went out. We were all standing in absolute pitch darkness and I had to cover my ears again to keep my eardrums from bursting. When the screaming went away, I tried to feel around for the wall but didn't find it where I thought it should be and I found myself falling down a short staircase, really less of a staircase and more of like just a handful of stairs.

I heard a door slam, and then the lights came back on. I was in a tiny room filled with video screens. On each of the screens was video footage of teen girls cutting their wrists.

This was very different from what I thought I was signing up for. I decided I had had enough so I started shouting, "I WANT TO GET OUT!!" at the top of my lungs. I yelled it over and over but nothing happened. I watched one of the screens for a second and the violence was just too graphic for me. I threw up on the floor. Then I tried screaming it again, "I WANT TO GET OUT!" Then the video feed flickered. It became static-y for a second, like the end of an old VHS tape, and then it switched to a live feed of the room I was in. It was really freaky, because the screens were on different delays so each screen showed me freaking out one to five seconds earlier. It was very hard to get my bearings. And then I saw it on one of the TVs— another person in the room. I screamed for a second and then I felt something heavy hit the back of my head. I passed out.

When I woke up I was in a different room where the lights were very low. It looked like a serial killer's basement. I was tied up and there were yards of duct tape wrapped around my mouth and head. I was starting to doubt that this was the standard package everyone who came to this "haunted house" got.

I tried to scream for help but it was hard to make any

substantial noise with the duct tape. Also, it was unbelievably hot. Hotter than in that meth room. I once went to a Korean spa and there was a sauna that was 170 degrees. I could only go into it for a few seconds, but this felt hotter than that. Out of the corner of my eyes I saw a man in a mask. He approached me, and held up a paperback copy of *The Shawshank Redemption*. He hit me across the face with it, a harder hit than I'd ever taken. The man took off his mask and... I couldn't believe it. It was Brett.

He held up the book and screamed at me, "You think I'm stupid, huh?? You and Hannah don't think I really read books! Well, I've read lots of books!"

He hit me across the head with the book again.

"I know all about what's in this book! It's about the friendship between a Black guy and a White guy in prison!"

Even as terrified as I was, I couldn't help laughing to myself, knowing that in the book it's actually two White guys. Even this book that he was hitting me with, Brett had only seen the movie. You would think he would at least read the one book he was going to use in this scenario.

But a second later, Brett was the one who was laughing. He had a knife out and he put it right up against my throat.

"Hannah is going to be mine again," he said.

And as he began to drag the knife across my throat, all I could think was one thing. "Man... dating is hard."

THE VOID

BY JOE CABELLO

"I'M WILLING TO do anything for this."

It was a sentence Cara had rehearsed a million times before as she'd fantasized about this exact moment. A sentence she'd repeated in the mirror over and over again, hoping to manifest her dream through sheer willpower and desire. It was true too. She was willing to do anything. Cara had been waiting her entire life for this.

To be a movie star.

Not just any movie star though. *The* movie star. A movie star so big, even your grandma would know her by name. Her face would litter magazine stands. Even the utterance of her name would illicit opinions. The internet would both love and loathe her, but one thing would be for certain: they would know her. She wouldn't just be Cara anymore, she'd be Cara Kaiser, and that would mean something.

The slug-like older man sitting across from her let his

pencil-thin lips curl ever so slightly. It was all he could muster for a smile after decades in the business. He had a nose like a pumpkin squash and the heft of a man who could afford a couple heart surgeries.

"Good," he rattled.

He was casting director Abe Gollup, a kingmaker in the entertainment industry. A green light from him would make her a guaranteed star. This meeting, her final meeting after dozens of self-tapes, in-person castings, and chemistry reads, would confirm her as the lead in the *Starblinder* trilogy. It was like a golden ticket to stardom. Just being in the running had already nabbed her millions of social media followers as well as several lesser movie offers. None of them would mean half as much as this one though.

After all those months, the role was almost hers, nearly confirmed in that very room as she admitted she was willing to do anything for the role to the one man who could give it to her.

Cara was driven, but she wasn't stupid. She had heard the stories about Hollywood. Who hadn't? It's not like it was Hollywood's dirty little secret anymore. Men used movie roles like bargaining chips to get whatever they wanted. At worst, it manifested in full on assault, at best, it was a morally ambiguous game of quid pro quo. Even if you were a willing participant, being so cavalier about your willingness to do anything for a role seemed like asking for trouble.

But Cara didn't care. This is what she wanted. Hell be damned.

Abe tapped his thick, crooked finger on the desk, like an oak branch knocking against the mahogany.

Tap. Tap. Tap.

Whatever it meant, Cara knew it wasn't as good as "you're hired." Her legs pressed so tightly against each other that the back of them went numb.

Tap. Tap. Tap.

Her palms practically oozed sweat. She considered breaking the vocal silence.

Tap. Tap…

His finger paused just centimeters from the table and he stared out at nothing. His lips pursed into a tiny subtraction sign. "Come to the Westin tonight. We'll finalize everything there."

Cara would have been lying if she said that her heart didn't sink a little. She was willing to do anything, but that didn't mean she *wanted* to spend a night in an old man's hotel room. She'd rather avoid it altogether, but her moment of disappointment was brief as she realized that if she was getting invited to the hotel, the role was as good as hers. A pulse of energy burst from her heart throughout her body. Goosebumps sprang across her arms. She could have screamed, but she didn't allow it. She was prepared for this. It was always meant to be, after all.

She thanked Abe with measured excitement so as not to embarrass herself, shook his hand, and quickly left, as if sticking around too long might make it all disappear. Once in the halls and out of sight, she jumped in the air like a child. She wanted to text. She wanted to tweet. She wanted to tell the world she'd done it, but she knew better than that. Even a cryptic Instagram post could jinx it. She couldn't risk that. Most of all, she wished she could tell her mom, who had passed away years earlier right when Cara had started her journey as an actress. Her mother's only flaw was that she never fully supported Cara's choice to become an actress, mostly because of the exact situation Cara found herself in on that very day. Even so, her victory made her miss her mother all the more. She missed her malapropisms, her peppered blonde hair, and the mole on the tip of her nose that Cara was happy not to inherit.

Cara spent the next couple hours eating an expensive lunch at Nobu that she unapologetically put on her credit card, and then bought a new ensemble for the night. Not just a dress. She went all out. Her shoes alone were so expensive that if the role didn't work out, she'd be heading right back to the store to return them. She spared no expense. She'd earned it. Black heels, earrings, a necklace, and matching bra and panties to go with her brand new skirt and lace top. She'd chosen the perfect outfit. Sexy and inviting, yet still leaving a lot to the imagination. The obvious choice would have been a cocktail dress, but part of the game was pretending you weren't going to play the game.

After her shopping spree, she went home, showered, and got ready. She did her best to avoid imagining whatever it was she would have to do, not that she fully stopped her mind from wandering, nor did her thoughts dissuade her in the least. She'd been ready since 5pm and the hours crawled until 7pm finally hit.

In the hotel's parking garage she performed one last check in her car mirror. Her make-up: impeccable. Her hands: steady.

Even her body knew she was ready.

As she walked into the Westin lobby she was immediately met with a surprise. Standing right in front of her was Luke Andrews. Everyone knew that if a studio wanted guaranteed box office success, they cast Luke Andrews. Few names carried as much weight as his. Reeves, Smith, Cruise,

Pitt. They were his only contemporaries. Not only was he standing in the lobby in front of her. He was looking straight at her, arms stretched with a big smile on his face.

"Cara Kaiser. I've heard a lot of very good things about you." He was even better looking in person, albeit much shorter. Five foot seven in boots. A smile so bright it could guide ships in the night, and a thick mane of black hair that made you want to run your hands through it just to make sure it was real. Most importantly, he had heard good things about her. *Luke Andrews* had heard good things about her.

She struggled with her words. "I'm here for- What are you doing here? I'm supposed to meet... what?" She caught herself rambling but couldn't quite stop herself. "I'm sorry. Its just, blah! I'm Cara. You're Luke Andrews."

He put his hands on her shoulders like a coach giving a player a pep talk and stared into her eyes with a toothy smile, "I know, I know. You're going to be a big star. I'm all caught up. That's why I'm here."

She pieced it together. "Are you in *Starblinder* too? I didn't know."

He shook his head, still smiling a toothy grin. Standing so close to him she noticed his teeth were slightly misaligned in a strange, hypnotizing way she'd never caught before. "No, no. I'm just here to help smooth things along. It's good to have someone here for this. Someone who's been in the same position as you."

She couldn't help but laugh. "The same position as me? I am nowhere near where you are. You're in, like, every movie. I haven't even been in one."

His smile gave, just slightly. "Not that. I'm talking about the void." He said it like it was supposed to mean something to her. He instantly clocked her blank expression and his face reddened. "My mistake. Spoke too soon. I thought Abe mentioned it already. You'll see." He mimed zipping his lips shut. "Let's go."

As she followed Luke through the hotel halls, she wondered what he meant by *the void*. Maybe it was one of Luke's new movies. Could she be getting another movie offer too? Then her heart pinged. What if she wasn't getting cast in the *Starblinder* trilogy after all? What if this was all for some other movie?

Their silent walk up to the penthouse ended after what felt like only seconds. Whatever was in store for her, it was right behind that door.

Luke pushed his keycard into the slot and the door beeped open, revealing a large living room where three men sat. One of them was Abe, which was no surprise, but next to Abe was Wilford Shalter, the head of a major studio. That studio wasn't even a part of *Starblinder*, even if Wilford Shalter was rumored to be the beating heart of the film industry.

If he wanted something to happen, it happened, no matter what studio was involved. Inversely, if he didn't want something to happen, it didn't happen. Shalter was a toad of a man who, despite wearing a custom suit, couldn't stop his bulbous neck from flopping out of his collar.

Most unusual of all was the third man. He didn't fit in with the others in neither look nor attire. He sat in the corner wearing a long, black robe turned grey and frayed with age. Deep crevices and pockmarks coated his face like topography, yet his skin had the sheen of porcelain. She didn't want to look at him but her eyes couldn't help but be drawn in his direction, like a gory wreck your body instinctively rubbernecks.

Shalter's croaking voice knocked her out of her trance. "Come. Sit."

She found herself suddenly nervous. She thought she knew what to expect, as bad as it was, but now she had no clue what would come next as she took a seat at the desk across from Shalter.

With all eyes on her, she finally remembered herself. "I'm sorry. Hello. I'm so nervous… I mean, excited, I've just been in a daze." The room of men let her words hang in the air without a response.

Abe didn't change expressions. She looked back at Luke who leaned against the wall by the door, eyes glued to the floor. Shalter's voice, like wet gravel, spun her head back toward him. "So you want to be a star?"

Cara was happy to have the conversation back on track. "Absolutely. It's all I ever wanted."

He smiled warmly for the first time, like he was lost in a memory, then his face dropped again as he continued, "There's a cost to fame."

Every sentence drew a long breath afterward, like he was straining under the weight of his bulbous body.

Cara jumped in, "I know, I know. My life is going to get crazy. I won't be able to go grocery shopping. I won't have a personal life. I won't be able to date. I don't care. I've thought about this my entire life."

Luke, suddenly behind her, planted his hand on her shoulder. "Just listen, kid."

Shalter took a deep, rattling breath. "I can smell the stink of obsession on you." He drew another long breath, smacking his gummy lips together. "I like that."

Her eyes searched the room to get a gauge of exactly what Shalter meant. Abe looked down like a sibling waiting for dad to stop yelling at the other. Luke did the same. The old man just stared at her with a grin, completely still, almost like he was just an image burned into her eyes.

Shalter continued, "You know the mega stars? The people the world adores? They get the love. The fame. The attention. People like Luke here. They all have a job they have to do to earn that. A job they have to do to keep that."

Her head swirled with questions, but she kept her mouth shut, not even sure where she'd begin if she did say something.

"The things they have to do… These are not nice things. They aren't fun things. They are what people do so they can *have* the nice things. The fun things."

She nodded as if she understood. He eyed her up and down, sizing her up.

"You really want this, don't you?"

She nodded assuredly.

He leaned forward on his elbows, suddenly looking like he wanted to get down to business. "Then you have to go into the void."

Her face couldn't hide her confusion. Luke jumped in before she could say anything, "Maybe it's better that she just sees it."

Shalter smiled a real, true smile. "Yes, yes. That's always better, isn't it?"

Luke spoke less confidently. "As long as you think she'll do it."

Shalter kept his smile, nostrils flaring as he sniffed the air in front of him. "She'll do it. I can always smell it on them."

Despite her excitement at the notion that this was all

really happening, the ambiguity put Cara on edge. Shalter lumbered up out of his chair as the old man hobbled over to them and replaced Shalter. He held his hands out on the table, palms up. Cara looked around for instruction. Shalter nodded for her to take them, so she took the old man's hands in hers. They weren't hot or cold. They felt like holding nothing, like the more she squeezed, the more there was nothing there. The strangeness of it sent a flutter through her body.

Luke whispered in her ear, "When you get there, you'll know what you have to do... You have to do it or this isn't going to happen for you. Ever."

"Go where?"

Luke sounded scared. "Just listen to me. Whatever happens... However you feel about it, this is just how it is. It's better if you just go with it. It's better than not having all of this." Luke quickly sat back down, as if retreating before Shalter could reprimand him for speaking out of turn.

Shalter casually popped a piece of gum in his mouth. "If you're ready to hit the big time, go ahead and look into that thing's eyes."

That thing? She thought as she turned to look at the Old Man. She caught his eyes, two little black dots. Everything else blurred under her intense focus on them. They were all she could see, as if they were growing and enveloping her entire vision. She felt like she was diving into the dark pools of his eyes. It made her dizzy and disoriented. Her eyes began to sting and water until she had to…

blink

When her eyes opened she was standing in a space of pure black.

A completely empty space.

A void.

The void?

Empty of all external sound, making her breathing blare in her ears like a blowtorch blasting on and off. Her heartbeat pounded like the sound of plunging in and out of water. Her panic manifested in a pinch in her chest and waves of heat rolling down her body.

"Hello?" her voice cracked. It had no echo. It just stopped, as if she were speaking to a wall.

Suddenly a thought popped into her head and formed into clear, distinct words, but it wasn't her thought, not her words. Like it was something she'd read right in front of her, or was whispered in her ear.

"I have to skin them alive…" She said. She felt compelled to speak it aloud.

Skin who?

She felt something in her hand. She looked down and inexplicably held a wooden-handled metal tool. It looked like a cheese grater. Jagged perforated holes in a slick metal surface. She held it up to her face, studying it. She ran her finger across it and recoiled in pain as dots of blood bubbled on her fingertip.

A guttural cry rang out to her right. She whipped her head around to see a middle-aged man strapped to a table. He must have been in his 50s. His otherwise kind features were masked by his sheer terror.

The man's voice was raw, like he'd already been scream-ing for hours. "Please, please, please, please. Help me. Help me. *Ican'tIcan'tIcan'tIcan't.* Don't do this..."

In utter shock, Cara stared at the man in disbelief.

"I have to skin them alive…"

A chorus of wails rang out behind her.

blink

There were suddenly hundreds of more people scattered all over the void. Men, women, children, all strapped down, writhing in panic, pleading to be let go. Her eyes darted around at all of them, no rhyme or reason to who all these people were. All of them different except for the one thing they shared: fear.

blink

Her eyes caught a woman in her 60s with peppered blonde hair, a mole on the tip of her nose.

Cara's mother.

Their eyes locked and for a moment, all the other people,

all their cries, disappeared. Cara's face twisted to horror.

Only seconds had passed for everyone else in the room when Cara finally opened her eyes. Her chest rose and fell with laborious breaths that she tried to stifle and hide.

Shalter spit his gum out into a napkin, throwing it on the floor. "Looks like we have our answer."

Cara stood up. Her voice quaked despite her best efforts. "How do you know I won't tell anyone about this?"

If the question surprised Shalter, he showed no signs of it. He simply replied matter of factly, "Who would believe you?"

She thought about it for a moment as her hands dripped blood and chunks of flesh onto the carpet. Then she nodded and marched to the door, stopping to turn back to them. "So, you'll send the paperwork to my agent?"

GREENTEETH

BY MATTHEW HARTWELL

SPRING

Stephen had told him to show up early the night it all started, and Danny didn't want to screw up his one chance, so he'd gone at 7, while it was still light out, and sat his stuff back far enough from the edge of the pond that it wouldn't get wet. Stephen said Kel and her friends were going to be there, which was exciting, but not as exciting as Stephen stopping by his locker that morning like they were suddenly in sixth grade again, and friends, ready to swap theories about whether or not Batman was really dead or if the cliffhanger that aired the night previous was just misdirection.

Stephen didn't want to talk about Batman anymore. Their Batman hadn't been on in a while anyway. There was a new Batman show, and Danny wanted to watch it, but, unlike Stephen, didn't have any younger siblings to help him justify it. That was fine. People change. He'd heard that. It's just that he hadn't.

Nobody had shown up. Kel and her friends ghosting wasn't a surprise - they probably went and saw a movie instead, or were over at Laurie's place, watching bad TV, or Stephen was misinformed. That was always a possibility. Some rumor half-heard and repeated, twisting until it was something entirely new, not real. But Stephen should have shown up. He at least thought the girls were going to be here. He believed it enough to tell Danny.

And then Danny heard voices. Not Stephen. Not Kelly, not Laurie nor the twins he could never remember the names of, Charlotte? Carol? One of them was Carol.

It wasn't Carol.

It was Luke and his friends. Mark and Nate.

Great, thought Danny. *Now I can get made fun of after school too.*

When they made him get in the water, he was glad they hadn't made him strip first. The water was colder than he expected, and his breath was visible in the air as he treaded. It had gotten deep just a few feet in from shore, which was almost as much a surprise as whatever fish or frog swam past his leg. They got bored quickly enough, which was a relief, as he had a stitch in his side already. When they left he started to quietly paddle towards shore. He could have gotten there a lot quicker with big strokes, he was a pretty good swimmer, but the less noise he made, the less likely they'd come back and be dicks some more.

He was almost at the part where the sheer drop off happened, where he could have clambered into the water and been just at shin height, but his foot caught on something sticking up out of the bottom. He yanked and pulled, but couldn't get free. Whatever had him seemed to tighten its grip. He held his breath and dove under the water to try to get his hands on it.

It was dark. With his head immersed, it was much colder than just a moment before and he shuddered involuntarily. He stooped over, his head a few feet under the surface and groped down his leg with his hands. He could feel it, hard and knobbled, twisting and knotted. It flexed a little bit as he gripped it, but it wouldn't untangle. It was a root or weed, strong and emerging from its home deep in the muddy bottom. It might belong to the tree his bag was sitting under, he thought.

He came back up for a breath and opened his eyes to see the moon above him. He inhaled greedily, and then yelled.

"LUKE!"

The woods were silent.

"LUKE! *HELP!*"

His voice echoed off of the pond, but the trees ate the sound. Nobody replied. He was getting tired. Adrenaline had not made the sharp pain in his side go away. He sucked down a giant lungful of air and headed back into the blackness.

He reached his foot and tried to worm his fingers in between the slick wood and his ankle but it was so tight, he couldn't make any progress. His lungs were burning. He was moving too much in his panic, eating up too much oxygen, he'd need to go back up very soon! He got a finger into the knot. He pulled, but it wouldn't budge. He needed more leverage. He wriggled it in up past his knuckle and pulled, and realized both mistakes at once.

Number one: he was pulling the loop tighter, not looser. Not a problem, though, as now he knew how the knot worked, and he could just follow the branch or root or whatever it was back around and pull the opposite way. Except for number two: His finger was stuck. His knuckle was too big to slide out, and he couldn't get it free. So he was stuck, bent over, underwater.

At least I don't have to get tired first, he thought. He continued to pull his hand, hoping to get it free, and slowly let a stream of air out of his lungs, trying to get rid of the carbon dioxide before it built up. It was a trick he had learned by happenstance, the summer before last, and he could buy himself an extra minute or two, that way. But his finger wasn't budging.

The pressure in his chest felt like it was going to burst,

and he opened his eyes, even though it was almost pitch black down here. Looking up, he saw the moon. And then a shape swam past it, briefly blotting it out.

Luke!?

He frantically waved his unrestricted arm, trying to get Luke's attention. He must have heard and come back! All was immediately forgiven. Granted, Luke's fault this happened in the first place, sure, but Danny resolved to forget that part. As far as he was concerned, Luke was about to be his new best friend, whether Luke wanted it or not.

The shape came back, it had seen him. It looked smaller than Luke.

Nate?

Nate was on the swimming team, Danny remembered. Obviously, he'd be the one to jump in. Well, he could be Nate's new best friend too.

Danny watched as Nate dove down further into the murky blackness and disappeared. He felt hands on his feet, undoing the knot. The pressure on his finger loosened enough and he shot up to the cold air. It was the best tasting thing he'd ever known.

"Luke! Mark!" Danny shouted at the bank, but didn't see anyone. In the depths, Nate kept working on the knot. How long had he been down there? He wasn't trapped, though, he could come up when he needed to, Danny knew. Maybe only

Nate came back, feeling guilty.

The knot came loose. Danny yanked his foot free and felt it come into contact with something soft and hard. Something like a head. Nate didn't come up.

Oh God, I've killed him. He saved me, and I killed him. Danny dove back under and felt around blindly in the midnight water. He found an arm and grabbed it tight, pulling it up with him. His hand fit comfortably around it, which surprised him, but as they neared the surface it tried to wrench itself away. He gripped harder, until the other hand came for him, squeezing his arm sharply enough to cause him to yelp out in pain. He didn't let go though. Drowning people often panic and can pull their rescuers down, he knew. They had gone over that in gym class. He had almost done it to Nate not sixty seconds ago. He pulled hard and brought him to the top and it wasn't Nate at all.

She was older than him, he thought, by maybe a year. Her hair was long and black and straight, though it was also soaking wet, and it was dark save the moon, now half-covered by clouds, so maybe her hair was brown and he just couldn't tell. Not the point. The point was it wasn't Nate, it was her, whoever she was, and she looked panicked.

"It's OK, I've got you," he said, as he pulled her towards the shore, but this only seemed to panic her more. She twisted again, and tried to break free, but he wasn't about to let his rescuer drown. She was probably in shock after he kicked her in the head.

Nice going, idiot, he thought.

He reached the shelf and hoisted his chest up over it for leverage. He heaved her out of the water, but she arched backwards at the last second and splashed into the pond. In his surprise, he lost his grip, and she vanished. Now he was panicked. He was coughing and gasping for breath himself and couldn't just dive back underwater to look for her, especially if she was panicking. She could pull them both down and they'd drown together, and he'd never even get to say thank you to her. Or screw you to Luke and his friends.

He dove anyway. Down to the bottom, and waved his hands around in a wild panic, hoping to graze her and find her in the unseeable depths. He came up for air, dove again.

Nothing.

He came up a third time, and she was there. Head above the surface. Well, kind of. Eyes just over the waterline, like a gator, but with her hair pooling around her, waving lazily as the water rippled. She went under briefly and resurfaced. Her eyes stayed open the whole time.

"Hello?" Danny stretched his hand out toward her.

"Hello," she said back.

"Are you OK?" Danny reached his other hand back towards the edge of the shelf and gripped it lightly with his fingers.

"Are you OK?" She hadn't moved. Her mouth was still below the water, he realized.

"Yeah, I'm at the edge. If you can reach me, I can pull us both out and we can go home," he said.

She ducked back under the black smoothness and appeared closer to him.

"Can you reach me?" Her mouth still wasn't visible, which Danny knew wasn't right, but also, couldn't really be bothered with at the moment.

Danny edged back towards the shelf and rested his whole arm on it. If he could coax her there, they'd both be safer. She stayed where she was.

"I'm Danny. It's going to be OK," he said. She moved closer, though he didn't see her taking any strokes.

"I'm Jenny," she said. She lifted her face out of the water and smiled at him with a mouth of sharp, green teeth. "You should go home."

She dove back into the muck.

SUMMER

Danny balled up the duffle bag to shove under his bed and felt something inside. He cringed and slowly uncrumpled the bag. He unzipped it, and reached his hand in slowly, as if he was afraid that whatever was in there might bite. His fingers brushed against canvas and leather, and twined around nylon laces. It was a shoe. Size ten, wide, check mark on the tongue. It was Luke's. He needed to get rid of it. Of *them*. Its sibling was in the bag too.

He could have left them at the pond. Jenny could have buried them in the mud, but what if they came loose? Floated up. Someone could have found one, and then they'd dredge the pond looking for Luke and they'd find Jenny. They'd hurt her; take her out of the water. Even if they didn't kill her outright, they'd put her in a tank somewhere and try to figure out what she was, but Danny knew what she was. She was his friend. She was his secret.

There were a lot of secrets now. Jenny had just been the first, though, granted, she was a pretty big one. Most people don't know somebody that lives in a pond in the woods who saved their life. Most people don't know somebody that is kind of more something. Most people have never seen someone get eaten, seen the look of confusion on their face when they first get bit, when they can't pull free from something, that is kind of more *someone*, under the water, when they lose enough blood to know they aren't going to make it, but not enough to be confused about who did this to them. To know it was you, and to hate you for it, but you know what, you brought this on yourself, Luke.

And Mark.

And Nate, though that had been tougher. Danny's memory had been right. Nate had been on the swim team, and he was actually a lifeguard at the local swim and racquet club. And, unlike Luke, who was easy enough to trick into coming into the woods by using the same story Stephen had told Danny, or Mark, who was told he could find Luke there, Nate had no interest in the woods or Mark and Luke. The night they left Danny there had changed him, though not enough to make Danny forget what they'd done. So it was a relief when Jenny told him they didn't have to bring him to the pond. She just needed to know where the pool was.

He took a screenshot of a map to show her, but that didn't help. The pond was her world, and little drawings of the rest of it made no sense to her. She just needed to taste it. So he brought her a cup.

"Gross. Chemicals. And pee," she said, after she spit out her first sip. Then she drank the rest and licked her lips and twitched her nose and Stephen fell just a little bit more in love with her. He had gone back the next night, after she had rescued him, and found her looking up at the moon. She had swum away to a safe distance, but he didn't leave. And he came back the next night, and the next, and soon they were talking almost every night, until she told him her problem.

About how hungry she was. About how it hurt to be so hungry, and how there weren't any fish left in the pond, because she'd been so hungry, she had to eat them all. And then the frogs. And now, whenever the birds would land on the water, or look for bugs in the cattails on the shore, she'd have to eat them. But they were so small. And her hunger was so great.

So he had decided to help her. He brought chicken at first that he had bought with money he stole from his mom's purse. Once his mom began to get suspicious, he smuggled hamburger patties to her that he had stolen from the school cafeteria until they started locking the walk-in during the day. But she was still hungry. It wasn't enough at once, she said, and her stomach was wracked with pain and she would double over in the water and sometimes, when she would look at him, her eyes felt very cold.

So he came up with a plan, and it worked, twice. Which was more than he had really expected it to, as proven by his inability to get Nate to go to the pond. So in July, when the heat was almost unbearable, and everybody was at the pool, he was startled, for just a second, to see her there too, swimming in the deep end, pacing under the high diving board.

That night, he asked her how she got there. If there was a drain pipe in the pond, tubes, tunnels, sewers that led to the pool, or if she had just walked there, but she smiled at him, with her green teeth, and reminded him she couldn't just get out of the water like he could. But no, there wasn't some elaborate system of pipes. No sewers.

"Water is water everywhere," she told him.

Nate was going to be closing up every night that week. And then there was a terrible accident with the filter pump, and Nate drowned, and a lot of him was missing, but even after they cleaned the filter and tried to reopen the pool in August, the mechanic was uneasy about how little of Nate had actually been in the filter. The man had told the police, and they investigated it, but there was no evidence of foul play. Nobody else on the cameras, coming or going, no footprints, no fingerprints.

But he'd still kept Luke's shoes in his duffle bag this whole time. Jenny didn't want to eat them. They were foam rubber and plastic and a hundred other indigestible chemicals that wouldn't be good for you, so he had taken them. It had been two months, though. Maybe he could just throw them away in a dumpster. Or two separate dumpsters. He needed to watch a few of those true crime shows his mom always had on in the background, but he guessed all those people got caught, so maybe they weren't the best teachers after all.

FALL

The leaves were all crumpled up yellow hamburger wrappers and nothing had turned red or orange this year. It was all yellows and browns and Fall clearly just wanted to be over so it could be winter. But at the pond, the leaves were different. All the green was gone, like everywhere else, but it hadn't turned ugly there. Some of the leaves there were a brilliant orange, like fire, falling downwards from the branches, or a flashing crimson, like ribbons on a present.

At first, he thought, she must hibernate over winter. Bears go a hundred days without food. But they're still active, even though they spend a lot of that time sleeping. And even every hundred days wasn't right. People weren't drowning here every summer. Maybe she was more like one of those salamanders he had read about. The ones in the caves in Italy or Switzerland or someplace in Europe. They lived deep down, where resources were scarce, and were all pale and cold to the touch, without any eyes because there wasn't anything to see. But she could see. She saw him that night. And she could speak, which means she had to have been awake or around people long enough to learn how to speak.

Maybe she had been a person. Maybe she had drowned and was a ghost herself, now cursed to forever be lonely and need people to drown with her. Except she didn't just drown them, he knew. She ate them.

Maybe she was a mutant, then. Someone had dumped radioactive waste, and she was a little girl, and had touched it, and it turned her into this. Or something awful had bubbled up from the rocky bottom of the pond, like natural gas, but with strange chemicals mixed in. She had fallen in and turned into this thing and lived here now.

But that wasn't right either. He had read about how great white sharks can go for weeks without eating, which wasn't a big deal, it seemed, in the animal kingdom. Heck, people could go for a month without food, as long as they had water. He knew that from Biology class. They needed minerals and stuff, sure, amino acids, potassium, sodium - the stuff that made the mechanics work, but calories? The body could live off itself long enough to find new food. That was the thing about the sharks that he remembered. The longer they go without food, the sharper their senses get. They can see better, sharper. They can detect vibrations in the water more clearly. Their sense of smell, already able to pick up blood in the water a mile out, increased. They could even read electromagnetic fields - the tiny twitching of nerve fibers in the muscles of other animals. It made sense; if you're hungry, get better at finding food. People worked the same way. He had read all about it in the library. Ghrelin, the hunger hormone, made you smarter. Cleared the fog in the brain, increased creative thinking. The first person to figure out how to use a spear was probably starving.

Was she like that? Had she been there, under the water, getting hungrier and hungrier, until she could hear everybody, just a mile or two away? The town springing up, everybody speaking English until she had heard enough gossip and se-crets and church sermons vibrating through the ground and reverberating in the water, and she learned it, just like a tod-dler?

The other alternative, which maybe scared him more, he wasn't sure yet, was that she was brand new. That she'd just popped up, recently. Spontaneous generation, like medieval people thought was how flies were made. Leave some meat out, flies will grow out of it. They didn't see the eggs being laid. Meat birthed maggots. Where maggots were, flies in-variably followed. Was the town meat? Did something leave whatever became Jenny here, deep in the water, waiting? He giggled at the thought of a Jenny-tadpole, flitting about in the silt, slurping up all her siblings, Jimmies and Jerries and Ginas. His laugh sounded slightly unhinged, he thought. Need to rein that back in. Stephen would notice a Renfield. A laugh like that was just a cackle away from ranting and raving and howling at the moon. He suppressed a snort at a little at the image of Jenny-tadpole growing arms and legs. Jenny-tadpole losing its tail.

Jenny-tadpole becoming beautiful.

Danny shuddered and pedaled his bike a little slower. He was in no rush to get back to the pond. Having a secret friend in the water who got rid of your bullies was fun until you started to think about where she came from. And why did she suddenly need to eat so much - a few meals in however long she was out there, at most, and now, just in the past month, how many pounds of meat? 300? 400?

Not meat. People.

But people were meat to her. Except him, he was a friend. But the others were meat, and meat made maggots and flies. Was she a fly? Or was she a maggot?

"You're being quiet," Stephen said, pedaling faster to pull alongside Danny. Maybe his laugh had just been an internal monologue, Danny thought.

"Just thinking," Danny said, and pulled away again.

They arrived at the pond and she was nowhere to be seen, which made Danny anxious. It occurred to him, not for the first time, that the past eight months had been a hallucination. A slow and steady break from reality, where he had done terrible things. He still had Luke's shoes in his closet, after all. Every time he got near a trash can, he pictured an unlikely scenario where they'd be discovered: a raccoon knocking it over as a cop walked by, a homeless guy finding them while dumpster diving and then being arrested, even one where he tossed them in unknowingly arousing a swarm of bees and attracting the attention of a crowd. So they stayed in his closet, for now.

Jenny emerged from the water, and Stephen was extremely confused, even frightened. Danny tried to explain what she was, and he calmed down a little bit as he wrapped his mind around it. He got super excited, and the three of them talked for a few hours, and then it came out what she'd been eating and suddenly Stephen wasn't as excited. He got quiet, and said he had to go and Danny had tried to stop him as he stood up from the water where they'd been sitting with Jenny. Stephen slipped and Danny didn't even think a rock that small could have hurt someone that bad, but it did, and suddenly his best friend wasn't moving. Danny had begun to panic, but Jenny knew what to do. Jenny was so smart, and so calm. She put her hand on his shoulder and he took a deep breath, tried to tamp down the feeling of panic rising inside of him.

But this was Stephen. They used to watch Batman together. He knew Stephen's whole family. He wanted to share his secret with Stephen, or at least, in retrospect, maybe just part of that secret.

Stephen shuddered as he inhaled, still unconscious. Jenny grabbed his legs and started to drag him backwards, off the shelf and into the deeper water, but Danny grabbed Stephen's arm. His friend wasn't dead. Everything could be OK.

Jenny started crying. He was going to tell people, she said, and they'd come and take her away or kill her. Danny promised to protect her. Told her he could convince Stephen he imagined it all. He told her he couldn't let her do this, not while Stephen was still alive, and there was a chance to save him.

She flashed her sharp teeth and blood streamed from Stephen's neck and flowed into the water.

"It's OK, now," she said. "We don't have to be afraid, anymore."

Stephen's body slid slowly off the shelf, and squelched as it was pulled through the mud, before it splashed and bobbed in the water. Then it went underneath.

Danny sat there and hugged his knees. He couldn't let her do this. He couldn't keep doing this. He was the one who had done terrible things.

He was going to fix this.

WINTER

The ice flexes and shifts as it's heated up just slightly by the first rays of the morning sun. Cool, blue light filters down into the water beneath, but fades before it reaches the bottom.

There, in the muck and the debris, on top of a pile of bones, fish and not-fish, she sits. She stretches up towards the light, smiles at how warm it feels. She's tired of the cold. Tired of the frozen ceiling trapping her in this jar. There's so much more water out there, she knows. So many places to swim, and love, and eat.

She presses her hand against the ice. It's cold, but so is she. Slick and smooth, she digs a nail into the surface and starts to etch out a heart. Her nail shudders as it drags against the ice, and she looks at what it says and smiles again. Jenny and Danny. She pauses, lost in reverie, and thinks about Danny. It will be nice to go other places, but it will be sad to leave Danny behind.

She swims back down to her midden and roots around in the pile of bones, fish and not-fish, until she finds him. She picks him up, and he's still smiling at her, a toothy grin, and she thinks back to the last time they talked.

"No, no, Danny, sweet boy. This isn't my home." She had smiled at him, she was suddenly sitting next to him on the shore. He didn't look up into the sky, chose instead to look at her, as she leaned in. He found the moonlight beautiful as it reflected off of her sharp, long, green teeth.

"It's just my nursery."

...THEN THE DRINK TAKES YOU.

BY GRAHAM STONE JOHNSON

MARK STARED THROUGH the windshield at the long stretch of blacktop his twenty-year-old Jeep Wagoneer was speeding down. The single broken white line passed below in brief sections, ticking off not only distance but time. He listened to the sounds of constant effort from the engine, the whir of the tires, the occasional blast of dust against the faded, chipped paint.

He paid attention to all of these things outside the vehicle because they were infinitely better than what was inside: three children, screaming in regards to their inability to share, and a withdrawn wife who occasionally screamed back.

The Jeep cruised past a weathered billboard for a watering hole named "Paradise," a "CLOSED FOR BUSINESS" banner pasted overtop. Mark let out a single chuckle at the irony.

"What?" asked Sandy. Her tone was one he knew well. It

didn't mean "What?" It meant "What do you have to laugh about?"

Mark sighed. "Nothing."

She stared at him a moment longer, her face showing clear disbelief, before turning back to her crossword.

Cross words, Mark thought, *how fitting*. In her defense, he knew he'd given her a lot to fight about. Far from a hero, he'd made a lot of stupid choices in the past few years. The worst of which was the reason they were on this hellacious journey, or "vacation" as they called it to their kids, in this rattle-trap of a vehicle.

Mark was an alcoholic. Clean and sober for six months now, he'd gotten back control of his life, but not before the serious damage had been done. He'd secretly drank away most of their savings over the years, was fired from his job, and had been unemployed for two whole months before Sandy found out. "Business trips" were really just weeks at hotels spent in oblivion, and it all added up to them losing their house. And then the newer car followed.

Now homeless, jobless, and short on funds, they were headed west to move in with Sandy's parents. His in-laws were kind enough to take them in, and for that Mark was grateful. But he wasn't looking forward to the humiliating condescension he was certain to receive on a daily basis from Sandy's mother. She hadn't liked him when he was gainfully employed, so he couldn't begin to imagine how she'd be now. Sandy's father would probably just avoid him, and Mark was fine with that. Jerry did like his whiskey though...

Mark's right hand instinctively went to his right thigh. Through his jeans, he could feel his six-month chip. He'd done this so often there was a ring worn into the material of every pair of pants he owned.

One day at a time... one day at a time...

And in that blissful moment of trying to avoid thinking about the indefinite hell his life was destined to become, smoke began spewing from beneath the hood.

"Aw, hell," Mark groaned.

"Recalculating!" blared an ancient GPS suctioned to the windshield. Mark paused it as he pulled off the highway, limping down the exit and into a run-down gas station. Its sign read "Phillips 66 - McClean's Cleanest Pit Stop! No better in all of Texas!" An old-fashioned bell dinged twice as the Jeep rolled to a stop by the pumps.

The station door swung open, revealing a mechanic as run-down as the place itself. Mark pulled off his sunglasses, popped the hood, and got out.

"Hoo-boy! Sure busted somethin'!" The mechanic spit, wiping tobacco juice from his jaw on the back of a stained sleeve.

"Very perceptive..." mumbled Mark.

The mechanic produced an oily rag and used it to raise the hood. He looked at the engine for an entire second before declaring his verdict.

"Radiator's kaput. Don't have any on hand, unfortunately. Can order you folks one, but it'll take time."

"How long?"

"Oh, three, four hours 'til they can deliver. 'Nother one or two puttin'er in."

Mark checked his watch. It was already past noon. "Think you can fix it before you close?"

"All depends on how long they take to deliver."

"There a place to eat around here? A motel?"

"Sure is! Both 'bout two miles off the main road, thataways. Can take y'all on up, you wanna wait it out there instead."

Mark nodded. "Just a sec..." He leaned in Sandy's window.

"He can fi– "

"–I heard." She forced her annoyance into a plastered smile before turning to the kids. "Pack up your toys, we're going to a motel!"

Mark sat in one of two chairs that passed for a waiting area in the tiny station, staring at the "No Service" banner on his phone. He slipped it into his shorts' pocket. He'd quickly changed at the hotel, due to the heat, and was glad he'd made that decision, as it was about a thousand degrees in the small room. He could hear the mechanic tinkering on another vehicle out back.

Looking out the window, he saw a dilapidated building across the street with a decaying wooden sign out front signifying something at some point used to happen there. He wondered how people could live like this. So devoid of life. So disconnected. So alone.

His eyes landed on the two magazines beside him. One was an auto parts catalogue, the other an issue of *TIME* from the Nixon Administration. He gave the latter a shot.

He must have nodded off at some point because the mechanic woke him to say the car was ready. Mark creaked his way from the chair and asked the damage, already knowing it'd hurt.

"Three-fifty."

Mark deflated and retrieved the credit card he'd used for the room earlier. He watched the mechanic run it through an antique card imprinter as thoughts of money brought more stress to the already stressful situation.

His hand went to his thigh once again, and felt nothing. Looking down at the worn ring in his shorts he realized in his rush to change he'd not swapped over all of his pocket contents. He'd been telling Sandy he was going to wait at the station in case the estimate was long. She didn't respond, just turned on the TV. He had gotten out of there as quickly as possible and must have left the chip in his jeans.

Damn...

That chip was in his possession twenty-four hours a day for the past six months. It was his lifeline. His protective Talisman. He felt naked, powerless without it.

Find a distraction... find a distraction...

The mechanic returned the card with a dirty receipt. Mark tried to focus on signing it but his mind kept churning, and didn't stop even as he exited the station.

Find a distraction... find a distraction...

He replaced his wallet, readied his keys, and found himself suddenly grateful to be in the middle of nowhere.

Find a...

He paused in the open Jeep door, staring across the street. The dilapidated building now looked relatively new, with illuminated neon in the window reading "OPEN." The wooden sign, no longer faded but freshly painted, advertised "Paradise Bar."

Shaking his head, Mark entered the Jeep. He finally managed to tear his eyes from the building, trying to ignore it, as his hand returned to his pocket and its lack of chip.

Mark stumbled from the bar, drunk, thinking about how he got here.

He recalled sitting in his Jeep earlier for a full half-hour, circling the drain, as his Monkey Brain and Human Brain battled it out. In the end the Monkey won, as he knew it would, by taking a cheap shot with an anticipatory Dopamine kick. So he'd chosen pleasure over pain and fished a quarter from the cup holder, called Sandy on the station's crackly payphone, told her the radiator was going to take a few more hours, then drove directly across the street. He sat behind the wheel, thinking that he could still turn back, pull out of the bar's lot, and go back to his family. But he was there, he was alone, and his Talisman was missing.

Now, sufficiently hammered, he careened the rest of the way to his Jeep and attempted the keys in the door before dropping them.

"fffssshhh–*ugh!*" He scooped them up on his third try.

Rising, he gathered his will to focus, but was easily distracted by a faint glow coming from the trees at the back of the lot.

He shoved the keys in his pocket and lurched toward the woods. Reaching the edge of the pavement he grabbed at a tree for balance, whiffed completely, tumbled ass over teakettle down an incline, and finally came to a stop at the bottom of the hill.

Mark sat up slowly, testing, not sure what, if anything, might be broken. Everything seemed fairly intact, but that could be the booze lying. He found himself on the shore of a lake, fog obscuring his vision beyond fifty yards or so.

He started to gain his feet but paused, noticing the ring of mushrooms encircling him. They varied in height and size, having rather large caps over their sturdy stems. He'd fallen into what his grandmother used to refer to as a "Faerie Ring." He'd only seen one before, as a small child, and hadn't thought of it in years. Only that one hadn't been nearly as large... or swaying... or emitting a bright green glow. Surreal sparkles drifted down from the rounded caps, fading just before they reached the ground. Mark gaped at what surpassed mere bioluminescence.

He might have lingered a while longer had he not suddenly recalled the day's previous events. Looking at his watch, he found its face entirely busted. He glanced at the sky, which had taken on an odd, ambient twilight. Rising awkwardly, and carefully, he stepped outside the ring of mushrooms. His grandmother had told him never to disturb a Faerie Ring, and for some reason, perhaps it was that weird, magical glow, he felt compelled to follow her instruction.

He proceeded to climb up the hill he'd rolled down, and after quite some time, he was nearly 40 after all, reached the top. Once there, he found nothing from the previous night. Instead of a bar, he was staring at a sheer rock cliff.

What the...?

Turning around he saw a massive ocean stretching off into a foggy infinity beyond the Faerie Ring.

You must still be drunk. Or unconscious. Maybe you're dreaming. Or brain damaged. You're still at the bottom of that hill and your brains are oozing out and you're going to die.

That last thought didn't frighten him as much as he thought it should, which was a bit frightening in itself. But the more he considered, he decided this didn't feel like a dream. He was seeing it from his own point of view for one, and his dreams were always in third-person.

He shook away the thoughts, looking back at the rocky cliff. High up in the side he could make out a small cave, light flickering from within. He considered it briefly. *The hell with it*, he thought, and found the first foothold.

"Hello?" Mark called into the cave. His hands were badly

scraped from the climb, but he'd made it, dammit.

He stepped inside, allowing for his eyes to adjust. The dim, damp cave was rather small. It had clearly been inhabited for quite some time, as tally marks, like those used to track the passage of days, were all that adorned the walls. There were so many of them.

Some pitiful attempts at furniture, roughly hewn from driftwood, were placed beside a small fire pit. Finally, Mark saw the scrawny, very wrinkly Old Man dressed in rags, sitting upon one of those pitiful attempts.

The Old Man tended the fire, where a tiny pot hung over the flames. He looked up at Mark, clearly shocked by his presence. The shock rapidly transformed into excitement as he leapt up, pulling Mark deeper into the cave.

"Come in! Come! Sit! I've been waiting a long time for you. Well, any you, I suppose! Any *one!*"

Mark followed and sat, uncertain, as the Old Man nearly danced around the cave, finally arriving back at the seat across from him. He smiled, staring at Mark, with eyes that had a certain green glow in the firelight.

Mark felt uncomfortable in the Old Man's gaze. "Thanks. I-I'm a bit lost. I fell down the hill... and the bar... this all seems... wrong."

The Old Man nodded vigorously and spoke at a rapid pace. "A bar! Interesting, very interesting! Yes, yes! That would fit the bill! Although it doesn't have to be!" He cackled unnervingly before continuing. "I've been alone for so long, with no one to talk to, ever since... well, since I can remember! But I'm very excited to have you! Are you hungry, uh--?!

"Mark..."

"Mark! Are you hungry?! Here!"

He scurried over with a bowl of soup, which smelled amazing. Mark accepted, surprised that yes, he was in fact very hungry. As he ate, the Old Man hunkered beside him, curiously inspecting his clothes, peering at his face, he sniffed.

"I'm guessing from your story... and the smell, you like the drink? That's your vice, is it?"

"Clean and sober... or was. Had six months. Then I blew it. Really thought I had it."

The Old Man nodded. A slight, knowing smile curled the edges of his lips as he ladled more soup into the now empty bowl. Mark motioned his thanks.

"Yup, yup, haven't we all felt that way, some time or another? Say, Mark... I'm a bit out of the loop... who's the President now?"

Mark scoffed. "A mentally ill, scandal-ridden, traitorous, failed businessman in love with Russia."

The Old Man blinked. He glanced at his tallies on the wall, confused.

"It's still Nixon?"

"What? No."

Mark returned to the soup, found he couldn't stop eating. The Old Man nodded, noticing the ring on Mark's left hand.

"You're married? For how long?"

"Been with Sandy for nearly fifteen years."

The answer came a little too quickly, too willingly, as Mark found himself unable to withhold anything from this stranger.

"Any kids?

Mark grunted an affirmative.

"How old?"

"Jenni and Sam, the twins, are five. Kara's seven."

The Old Man nodded again, thinking hard for a moment. "What do you do for a living?"

"Medical Sales."

"A salesman! Great, great, we can work with that…"

As Mark finished the round of soup, he was suddenly overcome with drowsiness. He clumsily dropped the bowl. It clattered on the rock floor as he slouched against the cave wall.

"Wh… what'd you do to me?" he slurred, rapidly losing motor skills.

The Old Man's demeanor turned grim. He stood, towering over Mark.

"Your life… so full of opportunities… so full. Family. A

second chance. But you made your choice. Chose you. Over them. Enjoy your new life," he said, as Mark drifted into warm, black, unconsciousness.

⁂

Mark woke with a start, and was relieved to find himself back within the circle of mushrooms. He quickly made his way back up the hill. At the top he dug in his pockets, finding the Jeep's keys in one and a single key on a motel placard in the other. He started the Jeep, put on his sunglasses despite the approaching darkness, and pulled out of the parking lot.

⁂

Mark knocked on the motel room door. Sandy opened it, half asleep, annoyed. She squinted against the evening light.

"Jeep's fixed," he said. "Let's load the kids and get back on our way."

"Why don't we just spend the night? We paid for the room, and the kids are already down…"

"I'd rather get moving, don't want to stay in one place too long."

She yawned, turning away. "Whatever, you're packing though… wake me when we're ready to go."

⁘ ⁛ ⁘

Twenty minutes later Mark pulled the Jeep back onto the highway, following the resumed GPS towards a new chance at life, merging into the westward flow as the sun slipped behind some distant mountains.

He drove in silence. Sandy and the kids were already asleep again. He looked at the children in the rear-view, one by one, as if verifying a mental checklist. Satisfied, he returned his gaze to the road ahead.

Sometime later, Sandy roused, rolled over. "How much longer?"

"Forever, I hope…" Mark said, thoughtfully.

She opened her eyes and looked at him. He smiled at her. She smiled back, despite herself, closing her eyes as she settled back into the seat. "Well, that's new… and it's too dark for those shades, Hollywood."

"Oh… hadn't noticed," he said, pulling them off.

A few minutes later, Sandy began snoring softly. Headlights from a passing car illuminated Mark's face. He glanced in the rear-view again, smiling at his reflection.

In the brief light, his eyes had a certain green glow…

The Picture

by Christopher L. Malone

ALTHOUGH HE WAS arriving noticeably late for work, John Steil still walked through the shop's heavy glass doors with a leisurely gate, convinced he hadn't missed anything. Tuesdays were impossibly slow, but no slower than any other day of the week during the off-season. Malatesta's Pizzeria did its best business only when it was swamped by little league teams and high school kids enjoying the freedom of Spring. Judging by the crisp November air outside of the shop, they were still many months removed from the warm weather needed to play ball, and outside of the occasional delivery or minor lunch and dinner rush, these days were mired in monotony. If variety was the spice of life, John's work was flavorless.

Nothing changed: The menu - same pizza options featuring flashy names for bland toppings, same array of basic sandwiches that were impossible to screw up, and same assortment of snacks deep-fried to the point of irrelevance;

The layout – same setup of booths lining the walls, with the same six circular high-tops at the center of the dining room; The music – some Top 40 channel that played the hits from, get this, yesterday AND today, clanged out from the shop's ancient sound system. They played the same fifteen songs seemingly on an endless loop, with mindless yakking from the DJs a couple times an hour. John felt like he had heard that one song by *The Spiral Dragons* one million times, the one about how she looked "*Diff'rent than her picture…*"

Even the bulletin board beside the glass double-doors was the same. Although the flyers themselves were always changing, the material posted remained static. The lost dogs who adorned their notices with endearing images of themselves were going to stay lost, and the yard sales promising spectacular deals for the early bird shoppers weren't getting customers on account of Malatesta's. The missing persons with pictures ranging from happy to troubled would probably stay missing, as their eyes gazed out into the same nearly-empty dining room that John saw every day, and the occasional Babysitter-For-Hire was not going to find work on account of advertising in this particular pizzeria. The board was always wall-papered in such a way that it all blended into one giant mess, and no new yard sale, dog, or face would ever jump out at anyone. John knew that, because he was the one who managed the bulletins, and nothing ever jumped out at him, either.

As he crossed the floor and side-stepped the usual chair and table placements, he glared at his co-worker Peter... *Peter*, who was absent-mindedly picking his nose as he stared at the buttons of the cash register, made John's stomach turn. He was greasy, unkempt, and constantly smelled of pizza dough. He had no discernable sense of humor, didn't like anything "too crazy" going on inside the shop, and was miserably inflexible when it came to scheduling hours. He was anal when it came to Malatesta's, too. He could tell you what was out of place at any time, anywhere in the shop. He knew how many they could seat at one time, and when the seating arrangements were botched by what he referred to as, "too many damn kids loitering around one table," he didn't hesitate to encourage the overflow to find a new place to sit. He probably even knew the name of every babysitter, lost dog, and missing person that littered the store's bulletin board. These weren't reasons to dislike Peter per se, but enough to make him fall short of enjoyable, into being merely tolerable. If there was anything that pushed the needle closer to dislike, it was the reality that John needed Peter to even originally get him the gig at Malatesta's, which could embitter anyone belonging to a job they hated.

He'd been in a bad spot at the start of the year, and Peter stepped up for him. The shop's original owner, Franco Malatesta, had just sold his business to Jamal Lawson, who owned the barbershop next door, and Jamal saw promise in creating a local hangout where everyone could be welcome, including the local disenfranchised youth. Peter was the lone holdover in the transition, as he was the only employee not related to Franco, and Jamal naturally selected him as manager to help keep things running smoothly. When the time came to hire others, John put in for a position, but Jamal initially looked at him with severe and untrusting eyes. He knew John from his early years, and had multiple times kicked him out of the barbershop for being listless or troublesome. It was Peter who convinced Jamal that John was more than capable and who would do whatever needed to get done, and his word was enough. For John, it was just supposed to be a short stint until something better came along, but lately it felt like he could be locked into this crappy job for good.

Peter thought that he and John were best friends, and worse than that, he probably wasn't wrong.

"Hey, buddy!" Peter said, smiling broadly while wiping his finger on his red, flour-stained apron.

"What's good?" John replied less enthusiastically as he walked back behind the counter to get his own apron and hat.

"Don't bother!" a voice called from the office in the back of the shop. The sound of Jamal's baritone voice and commanding tone always made John cringe, and he looked over to see him striding forward, the figure of an older man who hadn't quite lost the military build of his youth.

"What's the problem?" John asked, nervously, immediately inventorying the Rolodex of reasons as to why he might be so unacceptably late. As he hated his job, he could not afford to be fired, and he hadn't accounted for Jamal being in on a Tuesday.

"The *problem* is that you're late, *again*," Jamal spat. John grimaced, fully prepared to hear the worst. Instead, a stack of flyers was dropped next to him. "Lucky for you, we're not slammed right now, so you might live to see another day of employment."

John eyed the stack of papers on the counter-top; simultaneously relieved he wasn't being fired while dreading what he knew was coming next. "You gonna want me to do something with these?" he asked, hoping it wasn't what he thought it would be.

"Flyer run," Jamal answered. "We can't sell what they don't know we're offering."

Peter looked over at them cheerfully and piped up. "You're using my direct marketing idea!"

Jamal flashed a grin at his protégé and pointed a positive thumb in his direction as he glanced back over at John. "My man's got some big ideas, John! You pay attention, you might learn something from him."

John was less than enthused. "You mean another post office run? I just sent out mailers last week!"

"That's true, but this shop's been advertising using the same mailing list with little result, so Peter brought up going door-to-door."

"We made a new batch of coupon papers yesterday," Peter chimed brightly. "We've got a 'Day-Before-Thanksgiving' special that we want to push."

Jamal chuckled, clearly reveling in how clever he thought his manager was. "We're calling it, 'An Early Bird Special!' Get it? While they make their pumpkin pie, they order from us a pizza pie! We're going to pull in some new customers, but they got to know what we offer first."

He jovially approached John and patted him on the shoulder, gently turning him toward the stack of lime-green papers. "Don't just hit the nice spots, either. Door-to-door means *all* of the doors, understand? And don't take all day, either."

"Fine by me," John answered, grabbing the stack of papers. He was happy to have a reason to get out of the shop and away from its various smells. He popped in his earbuds and was almost out of the doors when Jamal's voice turned stern and cut through the music that had just started playing.

"Boy, get those damn things out of your ear!"

John turned to see his boss holding out an apron and a hat.

"But I'm just doing flyers," John replied. "What's the big deal?"

Jamal shook his head. "No music. Instead of that, you can say hello and listen to all of our customers when you see them walking. When you're on my dime, you wear the uniform so the people know who you are and who you work for."

John grunted, but resigned himself to the apron and hat, and he pulled the earbuds away. He tried to make it a point not to argue too much with Jamal, tenuous as things were. He put on his uniform and nodded to Peter.

"See you when I see you," John said.

"Have fun!" Peter replied, gleefully. There wasn't even a hint of irony in his voice.

The walk to the neighborhood he needed to sweep was not a very long one. It was just six minutes from the shop, but in the opposite direction from where he lived. Ignoring the directive to not take all day, he went with his usual leisurely pace, determined to milk the task for all the time he could. As he walked, he took on the childhood pastime of watching the cold steam come off of his breath, reminiscing about the days when he would pretend he was Superman, using his powerful ice-breath to freeze a bank-robber in his place. That in turn, made him think about the Black-version of Superman, *Steel*, who was even cooler because he was also named John, and without realizing it, his chest puffed up a little bit, echoing how he would pretend to be him as a kid.

"Those were the days," he muttered to himself, relaxing as he stuffed mailboxes full of his collection of ugly lime-green coupon papers. He had no intentions of knocking on anyone's door, but would certainly say hello to anyone passing by. In the November cold, however, there was no one out to greet. After finishing one block of houses, John glanced down at his cell phone to check the hour, and noticed that time itself had slowed right along with him, and it seemed like taking his time wouldn't take as long as he wanted it to do.

He trudged forward, block over block, stepping over countless cracks in the sidewalk, and eventually smiled at the diminishing amount of flyers he had left. There was maybe a dozen more that he had yet to burn through and he hadn't run into a single person yet. With luck, it would stay that way. He wasn't in the mood to deal with strangers.

The flyers thinned down to nothing. House 307's mailbox was the last one to be stuffed, and John gratefully crossed the street to walk back to the shop. With his hands shoved inside his pockets, he hummed *The Spiral Dragons* song…

"*Diff'rent than her picture…*"

When a terrifying noise broke the tune playing on his

mental jukebox:

WOOF WOOF!

He stopped immediately and froze within his path. A great mammoth of a dog was eyeing him furiously from the end of a short rusted chain.

"Easy, boy…" John said slowly, and he started himself on a sloth's pace away from the dog. It growled in response, and John went still.

"I shouldn't have crossed the street," John muttered. This wasn't his first time in the neighborhood, and although he'd never come face-to-face with this vicious beast, he'd always been wary of its tell-tale bark, usually sounding from the backyard of its home.

"Be cool…" John pleaded with the canine, but an even lower growl was all of the response he received, and John's fight-or-flight response kicked in. With caution thrown to the wind, he turned and bolted down the sidewalk.

If dogs could smile, then the beast chasing John was wearing a particularly malicious grin. As if it were a deranged game of Human Fetch, the dog sprinted forcefully after him, and a weak link in the rusted chain put up no fight whatsoever, disintegrating when the dog leapt forward. For all of his efforts, John's moves became one giant horror-film cliché. Not ten feet from where he had started running, John tripped over a break in the sidewalk creating zero separation.

He looked up from his point on the ground, just in time to see the dog begin to gnaw on his left ankle.

"Ow, ow, *OW!*"

The dog jerked its head from side to side, vigorously. It wasn't biting flesh anymore, but settled for the cuff of John's pants.

"Ugh, you bastard dog…" John seethed, trying to pull his leg away, creating an impromptu game of tug-o-war in the process.

A voice roared, "Spyder! HEEL!"

The dog stopped chewing immediately and bounded back over to the house and around the backyard. A small man with wild black hair that stuck out at odd angles under a trucker hat walked toward John and picked him up off of the ground. He wore a red hunting shirt and smelled like cheap whiskey and aftershave.

"Sorry 'bout that," the man said in a surprisingly husky voice. "Spyder's just excitable. Don't know no better."

Normally, John would've gotten in the face of anyone allowing their dog to use his ankle as a chew toy, but something about this particular man made him approach the situation differently. "I'm good, really," John said, half-assuring himself and half-assuring the dog's owner. He tried to appear convincing, but the hobble in his step gave him away, and the man steadied him.

"Nonsense," the man said. "Come inside. I'll have a look at it." Before John could argue otherwise, they were walking up the steps. He was firmly guided through the man's front door.

"You deliverin' pizzas or somethin'?" the man asked, as he helped John into what looked to be a living room of sorts.

"Nope," John grunted as he collapsed onto a plastic covered couch. "I'm advertising for the shop." As an after-thought, he said, "It's a direct marketing campaign."

"Hmmph," the man replied as though somewhat im-pressed by the lingo. He propped John's ankle up on the coffee table, rolled up his pant leg, and examined the bite. "Looks like your pants saved you from the bite breaking the skin. Shouldn't be nothin' more than a bruise." The man looked at John matter-of-factly, like it was obvious to everyone in the room that this matter would be settled quietly and without any authorities being informed.

No blood, no foul.

"You stay put," the man said with a hardened tone that John quickly understood. "I'll get a washcloth to wipe off the drool and give you some ice and a bandage. I think the sidewalk did more damage than the dog."

John just raised his eyebrows, as though in full agree-ment, and the man left into another room, leaving him to sit inside a stranger's house. A few seconds passed, and John began to stare around wide-eyed, taking everything in.

"Craziest five minutes of my life," he whispered to himself as he looked over the living room he was in. Oddly there was no television to speak of, which John had only ever seen inside his grandmother's house. In her house, she didn't have a living room, but a parlor, and children were never allowed inside. Maybe this was the same sort of situation, he thought to himself.

He looked around at the walls and thought they once may have been an eggshell white before fading to their current brown discoloration. The odor of stale cigarette smoke may have had something to do with it, and an ashtray full of assorted butts only furthered the suspicion. An old fake mantle place was stationed in the center of the wall to John's left, and like the coffee table beside him, it was collecting a fine layer of dust. A few pictures were scattered about, framed on top of the mantle and the table. One stood close to where John had propped up his bare ankle and he leaned forward to pick it up.

People's photographs were always curious things to John.

"*Diff'rent than her picture…*" he repeated in his mind, only semi registering that he was thinking of the lyrics.

He never hung anything up on his own walls, but his parents' place had them everywhere; evidence of a life that had been lived very well. This is how it always was with John, though. No matter where he was, be it a friend's house or this stranger's place, he couldn't help himself but to look at the pictures and knick-knacks in the room that he was in. He was just naturally curious like that.

The picture that he had in his hands now was a selfie, but the type that would make a person pause to look at it. In it, the man was posing with a woman who was probably his girlfriend. John stared at it for a second and decided that although he could see what the man was trying for, it didn't work for this particular shot. He looked like he was attempting that overhead shot where the camera's looking down, creating an image where all guys struggled to look confident while the women tried to display the perfect amount of cleavage, looking up in an angelic sort of way. That was the key to any great selfie - make it appear as though someone else was taking the shot while you just happened to be having one of the greatest moments of your life when the flash went off. With this particular image, however, it appeared that several things had gone wrong.

First, the man had captured the image with his forearm still lining the outside of the frame, which was the first dead giveaway that this was an ill-conceived picture. He also must have snapped it at the wrong time, because his face was half-pressed against the woman's cheek so that his nose was at an odd angle and you could only see one eye. He might've been trying to give her a sweet kiss on the cheek, but screwed it up on delivery, because his lips were slightly parted and pressed against her face in an awkward way. It looked more like he was going to take a bite out of her than give her a kiss.

As for the woman, she must've thought this guy's attempt at a cute picture was hilarious. Her dark brown hair was yanked back into some kind of ponytail, but he couldn't really tell. Either way, her forehead was exposed and you could see her eyebrows lifted all the way up to her hairline. Her wide-eyed stare was complimented by her wide-mouthed grin; the corners of her mouth were pulled so tightly to the sides of her face that her smile almost seemed unnatural.

John put the picture back down when he heard footsteps falling down the hall. The stranger came back into the room with a warm wash rag and began scouring the grime from John's ankle.

"Yeah, I'm gettin' a closer look at it now that I'm scrubbing all that dog spit away. Definitely didn't break the skin or nothin'." He looked up at John with a strong stare that warranted no response. "Let me get you that bandage real fast. It won't hurt to wrap it up."

Before John could argue or even politely decline, the man had disappeared from the room again. He had even left the warm washcloth to rest on his ankle. John should've left then, but stayed put instead, and quietly marveled at how the man had simultaneously lulled and intimidated him into a sense of security. Why argue? After all, it couldn't hurt to have the ankle wrapped up properly. Meanwhile, he could continue passing the time…

The framed pictures on the mantle all looked to be the same kind of weird selfies like the other one, with the exception of an old black and white photo at center that looked like it could have been a parents' or grandparents' wedding photo. John scanned the photos: were those the same girl-friend? Were they all different girls? They were too far away for John to really see intricately. If they were different girls though, the man definitely had a type… and he loved taking those selfies. He reached over for the picture by his ankle and stared at it again.

The photo looked stranger to him now. On second look, she seemed younger than he initially thought. He hadn't paid much attention to the girl's eyes previously, but now that he had, they looked like they had glass over them, like they were welling up with tears. Was she laughing so hard that she was about to cry? The prospect made John sit up and think.

"Whatcha got there?" the stranger solicited. John was startled and looked up at the man cradling a gauze wrap and an ankle brace.

"Just admiring your pictures. Sorry."

The man paused momentarily, looking down at John,

and for a second, his eyes intensified, as though he was on the verge of eruption, but then he let out a short grunt, dropped to one knee, and got to work on the injured ankle. In the awkward silence that ensued, John watched the man nimbly run the bandage around his leg, binding the brace to his ankle. His hands seemed to float about his skin, and they moved very quickly. Only once did John feel a heavily calloused fingertip graze the flesh of his calf, but it was enough to make his shiver in spite of himself, and John suddenly wished he'd never come inside at all. That's when the man spoke up.

"That's me with my girl, Connie," the stranger said, squinting at the picture frame as he got to work on John's ankle. "Know her?"

"No," John replied, feeling all the more awkward for being caught snooping at his pictures. He guessed all the photos were of the same girl. She must have changed her hair quite frequently. He paused, unsure of what to say, and after a moment added, "You two appear to be very happy."

The stranger gave another short grunt in response and did not look up, continuing to wrap the ankle. John noticed thick traces of dirt underneath the stranger's fingernails, and it made him want to look away, so he glanced back over to the picture in question, wondering if there was something he had missed. The man's grunt made John think that maybe they'd broken up and he gazed at the picture again to satisfy his curiosity.

Looking at it a third time, the two people captured inside the frame no longer resembled a happy couple. It actually seemed really uncomfortable. The girl's eyebrows were more arched than when John had first noticed. She had wrinkles at the corners of her eyes, which confused the entire expression of her face. Her hair was definitely pulled back, but it must not have been very neat. There were wisps of hair flying from the side of her face and it all looked very messy. It was like her hair was gathered up in a hurry.

John placed the picture back on the coffee table face down. The man unrolled John's cuff and patted him on the knee.

"Good to go. Sorry for any trouble."

Instinct forced John to smile at the stranger's apology. "No problem," he replied. "If you have some time, come on over to Malatesta's Pizzeria for a slice. That's where I work."

Why did I tell him that?

The stranger smiled and gave John a wink. "I catch your meaning. A dog bite ought to get a guy some business. I'll stop by and order a pie from you boys tonight. How's that sound?"

John offered him a hollow chuckle back and answered, "That sounds great, sir."

The stranger helped John up and walked him out the front door and into the yard. The dog, Spyder, had come around the house again, perking up when he saw John, but quickly cowering with his head down when he saw that his potential prey was being escorted by his master. The stranger walked John all the way to the sidewalk.

"You be sure to look out for dogs hiding in plain sight next time," he said to John with an air of authority that went unquestioned.

"Thank you, sir, I will," John replied as they shook hands and he began to make his way back. "Take care, now."

Although he walked back to Malatesta's with a slight limp, John's pace was actually somewhat quicker than it had been earlier in the morning. He called the shop on his phone to let them know in advance why he'd be late. Peter told him to take his time, but John could hear Jamal in the background, asking if he had upset the customer.

"Don't worry about Jamal," Peter's voice wheezed on the other end of the line. "I'll explain what happened."

"Thanks," John said. "See you in five," and he hung up the phone.

On the way back, he tried to hum *The Spiral Dragons* tune to himself, but couldn't concentrate. His mind kept going back to the picture of the stranger and his girl. *Or girls…?*

It was funny how he thought that it kept changing on

him. It seemed like such a sweet picture at first, but then not so much after looking at it again. The girl, Connie, didn't look comfortable, like she wasn't together. Her hair wasn't even pulled back right. What did she have holding it back there? Was it a worn rubber band? Why would she even let him put that picture in a frame in the first place? The whole thing just didn't sit well with him, but he couldn't figure it out. What was wrong with that picture?

"*Diff'rent than her picture…*" he hummed subconsciously.

He soon found himself in front of Malatesta's, his thoughts having made the time it took to walk back speed along. He could see Jamal rolling out some fresh dough while Peter tended to a customer, clutching a lime-green flyer. Direct marketing, indeed.

He opened up the heavy glass doors and went through, but instead of walking over toward Jamal to see what else he might have in store for him, John paused and looked over to his left. Something had caught his eye and his pulse quickened.

Face-to-face with the white noise of the bulletin board, a word inexplicably jumped out at him and grabbed his attention: MISSING

He searched through the large-type and bold print as if it was for the first time, really taking a long pause to consider the weight and finality of such a small word. He stared at it, and soon the girl's face surfaced from the chaotic void of flyers, the same girl, but different. In the shop's picture of her, she wore her hair down, with the loose ends limply hanging around her shoulders. The placid smile on her face communicated boredom, and the demure wardrobe combined with the picture's starry background suggested this was a yearbook photo. He must've seen this image more than a hundred times, and now he understood why the picture in the stranger's house was so wrong, and so terrifying.

John just stood in front of the bulletin board, entranced by the girl's eyes, bland and unassuming in this image, but glassy and wild inside the stranger's house just a few blocks over.

"What are you staring at, John?" Peter asked, having just finished with his customer, who sat nearby, waiting for her order.

"This girl," John heard himself reply in a daze, not bothering to look his way. "The guy with the dog, he said her name was Connie."

"Yeah," Peter replied. "That's what it says on the flyer. Connie Oates. We've had that flyer for months. So what?"

"The guy's got a picture of the two of them in his house," John answered slowly.

"What of it?" Jamal sharply asked from the back, hands full of pizza dough, impatiently breaking into the conversation. He was ready to give John a new assignment, but the look that John gave him when he turned away from the bulletin board was alarming. A light bead of sweat was forming on his forehead, and he looked weak, like he was ready to pass out.

"I think she was screaming." John answered. "He had her by the hair and I think she was screaming… I think they *all* were screaming."

How To Make A Ghost

by KATHERINE FORRISTER

How Do You make a ghost?

A grisly murder perhaps? A drowned child, a tragic suicide? Does the place of death hold power? An old house, a secretive forest, a cemetery for war heroes, an asylum once filled with children who never sleep? Perhaps the type of person matters. An old soul's restless heart, clinging to life, not yet ready to die? Someone lost and lonely? Abandoned? Unloved?

A person wronged, bent on seeking eternal vengeance?

Some living people swirl these ingredients like connoisseurs of fine wine, dissecting each aroma to find the true source. Sommeliers of slaughter.

Some light candles and hold séances; they clutch crystals and burn sage, reaching out into the unknown. Some grasp crucifixes and sprinkle holy water to dispel evil entities while praying for protection.

Others have honed ghost-making down to a science. They hoard high-tech equipment to track spirits, begging and pleading for them to speak. They chase tragedies like storm-trackers yearning for clouds to roll into a twister. The thrill compels them; the goosebumps tantalize them to seek dangerous paths. Yet, beneath their beliefs lurks skepticism that wraps them in a safe cocoon, so they are always surprised when a true ghost answers their call.

Abby Beauregard was one such person. She entered the house of the late Jacob Myers with a backpack stashed with scientific equipment meant for catching ghosts in the act. She had ticked off the list for ghost-making like a baker perfecting a recipe, like an alchemist mixing elixirs, hoping for miracles.

Yes, she'd decided. This trite, 1950s suburban house contained all the ingredients to produce a fantastic spirit. Jacob Myers' house was the perfect place to meet a ghost.

As Abby took in the canary-yellow facade with its big windows and bright blue door, she wished Ryan were here with her like usual. Before her brother had gone off to college last fall, she'd always crept in his shadow as they explored haunted locations with his ghost-hunting equipment that he had purchased off of eBay. She had always enjoyed the feeling of goosebumps frosting up her skin when she'd feel a ghost nearby, or when Ryan's thermal imaging device would highlight a stairwell as dark purple, meaning it was colder than the surrounding temperature (one of many signs that a ghost might be close).

Abby had finally grown more confident since her seventeenth birthday the year previous, during a party that had taken place in a haunted hotel room in Charleston, but some of her confidence was of the "fake it till you make it" variety. Then Ryan had revealed he'd gotten an acceptance letter from a college way up in Maine, and Abby wasn't about to give up their ghost-hunting hobby just because he was hundreds of miles away.

Now that he was gone, a painful knot tied up in her chest whenever she'd think of him. She wondered if he felt the same. Maybe ghost-hunting was a way to tie their knots to one another while he was gone. She missed him so hard, it hurt.

But she grinned all the same as she looked at the ranch-style house, with a second story tacked on one side. Because oh man, would Ryan be jealous if he saw where she was now.

Abby followed an elderly, but spry, real estate agent named Mr. Stephens past the open-ended carport and straight to the blue front door.

"You'll see once we're inside," said Mr. Stephens as he turned the key and opened the door, "that the family started some renovations before…"

"Before Jacob Myers committed suicide," Abby said, walking past him to enter the house. The temperature upped a few degrees, making her sweat, even in her blue tank top and jean shorts. She hoped the AC worked.

"Ah," said Mr. Stephens. Abby glanced over her shoulder and pressed her lips together to suppress a laugh. His large mouth was half-open, making his wiry gray mustache droop. He blinked a few rapid times as he fiddled with the jangling keys in the pocket of his gray slacks. He cleared his throat and adjusted his matching suit jacket before squaring his shoulders.

"Yes," he said. "But let's not dwell on that. Now here's the living room."

Abby raised her eyebrows. The living room was spotless, as if a 1950s homemaker in pearls and high heels had just vacuumed the mint-green carpet and dusted the clean-lined, mid-century yellow couch, walnut coffee table, and chrome television stand. Wood paneled the walls, and the window behind the couch was covered by flowery floor-to-ceiling drapes.

"I don't see any renovations, Mr. Stephens," Abby said.

"Oh, not down here," he answered. "Mostly upstairs, so far. Before the Myers family bought the house, it was practically a museum. From what I understand, the original owner's will ignored her family and left the house to the owner of a grounds keeping agency, said he could live here, but on the condition that he take care of the house and never sell the place. He never decided to move in, but he upheld the bargain of keeping the house tidy and preserved like a time capsule. But when his company dissolved last year, and he ran on hard times..."

Mr. Stephens shrugged and raised his hands at the empty house, now purchased and being renovated by the Myers family, about to hit the market next week.

He then waved his arm toward the kitchen, which was connected to the left of the living room. "The kitchen is largely functional."

Abby followed him, shifting her heavy backpack on one shoulder while a large canvas tote bag swung from her right arm, setting each of her steps off-balance. The kitchen counters and cabinets formed an L shape, with a bulbous, bright yellow refrigerator tacked on one end. The lower cabinets were painted a matching daffodil shade, but the upper cabinets were a bold, mint green. Two wicker chairs flanked a small breakfast table.

The yellow-and-gray-checkered linoleum floors looked freshly-mopped, almost too clean.

"I'm told the oven is on the fritz," Mr. Stephens continued, "but someone your age is more likely to use the microwave, am I right?" He winked at Abby, which added a brand new series of wrinkles to his road-map face.

"Sure," Abby replied, not bothering to argue with the old man about the capacities of teenage-hood. Besides, it would be a miracle if the microwave worked at all. It was the size of a normal oven, mounted into the wall, and looked like some supercomputer science experiment with huge temperature gauges and dials. Abby felt like an archaeologist unearthing fossils in this unchanged 1950s house. She wondered what she would discover next.

Mr. Stephens dropped a set of keys onto the white laminate countertop. "Front door and back door," he said, "but I don't think you need to be going out back. There was a tool shed in the yard that... well, it's not standing anymore. So, don't go poking around out there; it could be dangerous. Splinters, uneven ground..."

"What happened to it?" Abby asked.

"Fell down, that's all." He pulled out an old-fashioned handkerchief from his jacket and started dabbing beads of sweat from his tawny forehead. "This whole house was built in 1956, after all. Which is why you need to be extra careful, especially in places the Myers family started renovating. The upstairs bathroom is completely gutted, so you'll have to use the downstairs one. There's no cable or internet, either. You brought some entertainment for the week, I hope?"

"Plenty," Abby said with a smile. She waved her phone

at Mr. Stephens. "And if I get bored, I've got this." She lifted her elbow to display the dangling canvas tote.

He frowned. "What is all that? Yarn?"

"Knitting," Abby answered. Her canvas tote was brimming with big, fluffy balls and skeins of multicolored yarn, with two long wooden knitting needles poking out like porcupine quills.

"Knitting?" he laughed. "Aren't you a little young for such an old-school hobby?"

"It's trending," Abby said with a shrug that made her shoulder hurt from her heavy backpack, filled with all her clothes and toiletries, not to mention bits of ghost-hunting equipment stuffed in the crannies. She wasn't about to let Mr. Stephens know what all *that* was. He hadn't responded well to her questions about the late Jacob Myers. Ghost-hunting might prompt him to tell the Myers family how weird she was, which might make them change their mind about hiring her as a house-sitter for a week.

"I learned from YouTube. Passes the time." She beamed a disarming smile.

"Well, all right," Mr. Stephens said with a nonplussed grin. "Knitting, it is." He crossed the kitchen and gestured her down a narrow hallway. "Let me show you the rest of the house."

She followed him down the hall, peeking through two

doorways that showed small, unfurnished bedrooms. The end of the hallway opened up into a white-painted, brick-walled mudroom with a glass door leading out to the back-yard, though heavy floral drapes were drawn across all but the edge. A curved wooden staircase led to the second floor on the right. Each stair had a big gap of space underneath, wide enough to stick a foot through if Abby didn't watch her step. The staircase was lined by a narrow wooden railing, with a series of thin, straight balusters that looked like you could knock them down with a single kick.

"You sure this is how you want to spend your spring break?" Mr. Stephens asked as they ascended the creaking stairs. "You're a senior, right? Last big chance to hang out with your friends before graduation. My son's a junior; he's camping two hours north in Blueridge. Prettiest place in Georgia, they say."

"Don't worry," Abby said. "I'm not going to throw a house party or anything. I'm good with peace and quiet."

He eyed her as she reached the top of the stairs, but she maintained her innocent smile, aided by her winsome ba-by-face with two little dimples that made people think she was younger than she was. He seemed to buy it.

"That's the gutted bathroom you can't use," he said, nod-ding to a doorless room down the short, loft-style hallway. "And here's the master."

He showed her into a bedroom with wood-paneled walls and a single window that faced the street, half-covered by floral drapes. An old vanity shared the wall with the window, with a chair tucked under the edge, though a mirror was absent from its oval wooden frame. The double bed sported a cushioned, emerald-green headboard with big buttons in every quilted crater. A nightstand supported a lamp shaped like a porcelain cat. All looked clean, though a little dusty.

"Is this where Jacob Myers stayed?" Abby asked as her heart sped up, feeling a little spooked as she imagined curling up under the frayed pink quilt.

"Yes, it is, but don't you worry about that," Mr. Stephens said. "I'm sure you'll be comfortable in here. It's the only room with a bed, as you saw."

Abby nodded. She set down her backpack and tote bag on the beige carpet near the vanity. The vanity's surface was bare, aside from a jewelry box made of wrinkled cream leather with a dainty brass handle.

She frowned in curiosity as she saw a single playing card sticking out from under the jewelry box, face down. She slipped it out and turned it over. A jack of spades.

She glanced around for any others, but the jack seemed to be alone.

"Oh," Mr. Stephens said, sounding uncomfortable. Abby looked up and raised her eyebrows at the grimace he was aiming at the card. "Police must have missed that one."

"What do you mean?" Abby asked. Mr. Stephens' brown skin had turned a little ashen, but he shook his head and waved his hand at her like a white flag of surrender.

"Well, since you seem so interested," he said, rearranging his suit jacket and lowering his backside to the corner of the bed before he seemed to think better of it and stood. "A couple of weeks after Jacob Myers moved in, a neighbor, Mrs. Carter, called about the shed caving in out back. When the police came, they found this house filled to bursting with playing cards like that one. Except most of the cards were stacked up into houses. Dozens of houses of cards, some big, some small, under the bed, on the kitchen table, some stacked floor to ceiling. Jacob Myers was obsessed. I saw some photos and, well, I've never seen anything like it."

Abby frowned at the card. The jack's face leered at her; each black spade looked sharp and dangerous. She suppressed a shiver and tucked the card back under the jewelry box.

"So... how did he go?" she asked. "Jacob Myers? He built a bunch of card houses and *then*...?"

Mr. Stephens squeezed his handkerchief and rubbed his other palm on his thigh. "Don't know why you're so morbidly curious when you're staying here alone all week. Gives me the creeps."

"Please—"

Mr. Stephens raised his hands as if talking her down, "All right, all right. Long as you promise not to go pokin' round that tool shed." He sat on the edge of the bed for real this time and braced his hands on his thighs. He leaned forward.

"Jacob Myers made his own grave," he said, his voice hushed with sensationalism as if his reluctance to share the details had burst through a dam.

Abby's heart thudded. "What?"

"No one knows what made him do it, but he left a scrap of paper with a note. *'Something's wrong. Goodbye.'* That was it. After Mrs. Carter's noise complaint, what the police found... Well, they say he must have been trying to build a shed, but instead, he built himself a death trap. Would have been ruled an accident, 'cept for the 'goodbye' note."

"A death trap? How?"

"He was using all kinds of wood out there; plywood, two-by-fours, posts. He dug some supports in the ground," Mr. Stephens held up one finger in emphasis. "With a spade, mind you, that's the only tool they found out there; not a shovel, a little *spade.* Then he arranged all the pieces of wood so they propped one another up like some big Tetris puzzle. He made a whole little building that way. But... there was no door. He built himself into the shed, and the police say there wasn't a single nail or screw holding any of it together. He'd achieved this perfect balance, you see, but it all came down to this one wooden post standing in the middle, supporting the ceiling. All Jacob Myers had to do was kick it down. That's what they say he must have done. He knocked out that post and..."

Mr. Stephens made a crashing noise and waved his hands in a mini explosion. "The whole shed came tumbling down. Crushed him."

Abby listened with an open mouth and wide eyes. "That's incred... I mean, that's awful. Just horrible."

Mr. Stephens nodded with a grim frown. "So, you satisfied, little lady?"

Abby swallowed and brushed a frazzled strand of auburn hair away from her face and tucked it back into her single braid.

"The neighbor," she said, causing Mr. Stephens to sigh with impatience. "Mrs. Carter? She was the same old neighbor who called in the first owner's death, right?"

"Now, how do you know about that?" Mr. Stephens asked, tilting his head with a shrewd gathering of his eyebrows.

Abby slipped her hands into her slim shorts pockets. "I read an old newspaper. A widow, Samantha Witherton, lived alone in this house after her husband died in 1958. She was a hypochondriac. Always calling ambulances and having doctor's appointments every other week for no reason, completely obsessed. Even her grown-up kids stopped visiting cause they wouldn't put up with her anymore. Maybe that's why she didn't include them in her will, like you said. The newspaper said she overdosed on pills, right? Did she sleep in here, too? Did she *die* in here?"

Mr. Stephens tucked his balled-up handkerchief back into his jacket with a frown.

"As a real estate agent, you have to disclose deaths in the house, right?" Abby pressed.

"For prospective owners," he said, standing. "Not for curious, house-sitting teenagers. If we're done with the interrogation, I'd like to get on with my afternoon."

"Yeah, sorry," Abby said. "I was just... curious."

Mr. Stephens left the bedroom and paused at the top of the curved staircase. He leaned on the top railing. It creaked and bowed a little, and he stood straight.

"You be careful, now," he said, looking down at the twelve-foot drop into the mudroom. "Like I said, this house is old."

"I will. Thanks, Mr. Stephens."

"The Myers family plans to flip this place as soon as possible. That was the plan all along; now they're even keener on it happening fast, as you can imagine. So, keep it nice and neat, don't let any vandals in, and all should go just fine."

The tool shed was in shambles.

The late afternoon sun cast long, thorny shadows from spikes of splintered two-by-fours, and glinted off a pile of nails on a stepping-stone nearby. Black shingles glittered and draped over split plywood like old curtains.

According to Mr. Stephens, Jacob Myers had never used any nails or screws, whatever his original intentions may have been. All his varied pieces of wood had been cleared aside by the police to expose a shallow, rectangular hole in the dirt. Maybe Jacob had dug it in preparation for pouring a concrete foundation, but it was the perfect size for a man to lie down in, like a shallow grave.

Abby wiggled out her excited energy as she clutched her phone to her chest. Even if Jacob Myers' body wasn't still in that grave, maybe his ghost... lingered.

She raised her phone and aimed it at the scattered rubble.

Ryan had given her a birthday present last year that made her squeal like a little girl and hug him so tight he'd had to pry her off him to breathe. The gift was a little black box that could snap into her phone to turn the camera into a high-tech thermal imaging device. It was way more expensive than any of the equipment she'd scraped up funds to buy herself, but after this house-sitting job, maybe she could afford even more equipment, like a state-of-the-art night-vision camera, a set of dowsing rods like Ryan's, or an EMF meter for her next adventure.

Abby grinned as she thought again of how jealous Ryan would be when she told him about this lucky find. Because, unlike most places they had ventured before, Abby had this treasure-trove all to herself.

They'd started their ghost-hunting journey in Savannah when they'd gone on a "ghost tour" through the city. The tour guide had said that Sherman's March to the Sea during the Civil War had turned the coastal city into a haven for ghosts. Sherman had converted hotels into hospitals for soldiers, many of whom had died within the walls, and since the city was one of the most historic in Georgia, it had collected all sorts of other spirits throughout the years.

The tour had stirred a morbid excitement in Abby. She imagined what it would be like to see and understand otherworldly concepts that other people couldn't. She dreamed that maybe, she could be *special* enough to be chosen by a ghost, that she might discover what lay *beyond*. More so, she wondered how it would feel if she were the first person to ever find definitive proof that ghosts were real. She would be famous.

Despite the truth of some of the tour guide's claims, Savannah was a tourist trap. Hotels would rent out their "most haunted rooms" to anyone who could pay. The ghost tours were sensationalized, and they restricted where you could go. Abby and Ryan had branched out after that, trying to find the most haunted places in Georgia and meeting up with other ghost hunters both online and in person to swap stories of off-the-beaten-path locations.

That was how Abby had found this place. She'd been scouring the internet for spring break ideas, and here, only forty minutes from her house in Smyrna, was a house with two untimely deaths, reports from the neighbor, Mrs. Carter, of strange paranormal activity, and an open advertisement for a house-sitter while Jacob Myers' family worked on real estate details to get the house ready for market.

That's why Jacob Myers had been here in the first place. He was in the process of fixing up the house when *something* had apparently made him snap. The family had refused to step foot in the house after Jacob's death. They hadn't disclosed why, but Abby hoped... *hoped*... it was because they knew the place was haunted.

Haunted by the old widow who overdosed, Samantha Witherton? Haunted anew by the suicidal Jacob Myers? A delightful dual haunting?

Abby was determined to find out.

She looked at her phone screen, covered in yellow, orange, and red splotches that formed the shapes of the rubble of the shed, the stepping-stones leading back to the house, and the bushes lining the fence around the yard. In thermal imaging, the spectrum from yellow to red represented heat. The visual range of the camera could then descend into shades of blue and purple, all the way to almost black to represent cold temperatures. Today was warm and sunny, so most of the yard looked yellow and orange, with a splotch of bright reddish-blue in the shade under an oak tree.

Often, spirits would manifest outside of the ranges of human sight, but they would be detectable by their chilling presence. Abby pushed record and took slow, steady steps as she panned the camera all around. She kept her eyes strained on the screen, searching for any patches of blue or purple that would denote unexplainable cold spots. She felt the jumpy need to look everywhere at once, but she couldn't risk missing something that only the camera could catch. She could watch the recording later, over and over to search for signs, but she wanted to see it live. She could react to it live.

Her heart beat faster as she crept closer to Jacob Myers' death-trap shed. Her stomach felt hard and tight as she approached the shallow crater in the middle of the rubble that she had now convinced herself was a grave. She imagined what she would do if a ghost popped out of the hole, and pressed her tongue to the roof of her mouth to stop a potential scream should anything unexpected happen.

The thermal imaging colors of the grave's edges shifted from red to a slight blue tint. Abby reminded herself that a small color change was normal. The grave was shallow, but surrounded by cold earth. A sign of Jacob Myers' lingering spirit would have to be a dramatic change. Dark navy blue, at the least. A dark, deep purple would be a sure sign.

Abby had never seen a change that drastic in any of her ghost hunts with Ryan, except once when they had later discovered it was due to a sudden rush of air-conditioning. But there were plenty of stories of people who had experienced ghosts through thermal imaging, and Abby believed them.

Abby paused at the edge of the hole. She swallowed and aimed her camera straight at the bottom of the grave.

She felt a surge of relief that she tried to dampen when the color didn't change. She *wanted* to find a ghost, so she should be disappointed, not relieved. She took a deep breath and waited to see if the reddish-blue would deepen into purple. Nothing happened. She peered around her phone to see the hole with her naked eyes. Roots from the oak tree writhed through straight spade-marks along the Georgia red clay sides. That kind of digging would have taken some doing; that clay could be hard as cement, depending on the weather. Mr. Stephens said Jacob Myers had used a small spade, rather than a shovel. He must have been *very* determined.

Abby shuddered and lifted her camera above the grave, and then spun in slow circles before wandering the yard, but no evidence of ghosts showed up.

She stopped walking when she felt a hard point under her tennis shoe. She raised her foot and saw a nail sticking out of the thickest part of her leather sole. She scowled and plucked it free, then swiped off her camera. The sun was setting; she'd had no luck in the yard for nearly an hour.

She headed back up the stepping-stone path and pulled aside the glass door. The house was hotter than outside, but still not a drastic temperature shift that might reveal a ghost.

As night deepened, Abby's resolve to hunt for a spirit snapped into jumpy fear. She got a window-unit AC going, but every renewed blast throughout the ensuing hours made her freak out about the source before she remembered what it was. Every creak of the floor and rustle of the wind outside made her less and less keen on discovering a spirit. She told herself that she was being ridiculous; she had signed up for this job to find a ghost.

She started to feel like she couldn't do it without her big brother's arm to grab onto, or without his reassuring voice when she began to panic. She told herself that all she needed was to get acclimated. As she hopped on her phone to grasp for the outside world, scrolling through Instagram, watching the new *Starblinder* trailer, and laughing at videos of her friends dancing to the newest *The Spiral Dragons* song, she promised herself that tomorrow night would be better. She would be braver.

Even so, all Abby could think of was the disappointment of calling Ryan with no news. If he were here, they would talk about a fresh plan on where to look next, what new tool from his fancy kit they could use, or they would rehash the entire background story of the "case" to look for new clues they might have missed.

But Ryan was a bookworm and probably studying for some big college test. She couldn't risk interrupting him unless she had some actual evidence to discuss. His spring break was in a couple of weeks; if she found nothing in this house, she could discuss her uneventful experience with him then.

Abby sat up in bed. A heavy, oppressive weight shrouded her on all sides. Each breath felt tight, and she had to force herself to deepen her next inhale so she felt less dizzy when she exhaled. Her thin cotton T-shirt and pajama shorts were soaked with sweat, and her hair felt damp. She looked around her dark room with wide eyes, wondering what had awoken her when no signs of dawn filtered through the blinds of the bedroom's single window. The only light came from a streetlamp outside, glowing from several houses down.

She heard a light rattle, like someone had shaken a maraca. She thought she heard a distant cough next, but as her eyes searched the darkness, she got the distinct feeling that the cough and rattle had come from the opposite corner of the bedroom. A dark blackness emanated from the corner, like a shadow's shadow.

Abby's throat constricted, and her hands felt clammy. She felt frozen in bed, unable to look away from the corner. She strained her eyes, trying to make anything out of the blackness, but that was all there was. Oppressive, dread-inducing, heart-crushing darkness.

"H—hello?" Abby said, her hoarse voice hitching. She thought she heard an echo of her attempt to speak, like someone trying to suppress a cough.

Abby's muscles jumped like electric wires as she latched onto a rush of willpower to grab her phone from the nightstand. She opened the thermal imaging app and aimed her phone's camera at the corner.

There was nothing there but the standard orange of the not-quite-air-conditioned-enough room. No temperature descent into blue or purple blobs. No opposite signs of hottest yellow. No signs of a spirit. She swiped open her phone's normal camera and started taking photo after photo. Nothing abnormal showed up—no spirit orbs, no ethereal shapes of figures, no flashes of movement across the screen.

She lowered her trembling arm and reached for her EVP scanner on the nightstand instead. An EVP (electronic voice phenomena) radio frequency sweep scanner, also known as a "spirit box," was another prime tool in any ghost-hunter's repertoire. The spirit box was small and rectangular, with a black plastic finish and glowing red numbers that displayed the radio frequency. A big round speaker took up the left half, and multiple red buttons allowed Abby to scan backward and forward across frequencies, and to record all audio so that she could play it back later at different speeds to listen for any ghostly words pushing through the static.

She turned on the spirit box and tried to silence her shaky breaths, listening through the static for the coughing, the maraca rattling, the throat clearing. She couldn't hear anything except the white noise of static as the scanner swept across uninhabited FM and AM radio frequencies. She'd saved up for a good quality one with a Faraday-lined wallet that would block out music and talk-radio stations, giving the spirits an opportunity to use the energized medium to speak. But no ghost seemed to want to speak now.

Then, the dread relinquished. Abby took a freeing breath as if binding chains had broken loose from her body. Without warning or explanation, the deep blackness dissolved. Dim light from the streetlamp stretched into the corner, illuminating nothing but carpeted floor and a plain wall. A single cobweb stretched between the walls across the ceiling.

But sleep had fled with no hope of return. Abby's heart hammered, and she couldn't catch her breath. She left the EVP scanner on, set to record audio, and pulled a beaded chain on the porcelain cat lamp. Light spread like a sunburst around the room that now looked completely normal, though Abby couldn't help but look at the jack of spades playing card on the vanity. Its corner was still tucked underneath the old jewelry box.

She swung her feet off the bed and forced herself to walk across the room to the vanity, keeping the empty corner of the room in her peripheral vision as if a coiled cobra might strike. She hovered her hand over the playing card, but she couldn't bring herself to break through the charged energy that seemed to tingle the air between the jack's leering face and her fingertip.

She flung open the lid to the jewelry box instead. It was lined with rose-colored satin, dotted with a gold pattern that looked like tiny, stylized atoms. Yet it wasn't filled with jewelry. The box was brimming with small, clouded-glass bottles. They were coated in dust and wrapped in faded and frayed paper labels. Some were filled with varying amounts of liquid; others held what looked like a collection of pills.

She narrowed her eyes, trying to read some of the labels.

Milk of Magnesia. Ritalin. Cough Syrup. Petro-Syllium. Antibiotic Throat Lozenges. Snake Oil. Aspirin. Fastabs. Placydil.

She picked one up that had no label at all.

It rattled.

She dropped the bottle back into the jewelry box. She closed the lid and darted back, shaking.

Rattling pill bottles. Distant coughs and clearing of a throat... Could the darkness that had inhabited the corner be the spirit of the old hypochondriac woman, Samantha Witherton?

"OK," Abby whispered, letting out a slow breath through pursed lips. She took another deep breath, grabbed the pink-cushioned chair from the vanity, and carried it to the barren corner. She set it down, facing the bed, and retrieved her canvas tote bag filled with yarn and knitting needles. She sat down in the chair with the bag in her lap.

For a moment, she sat there breathing in and out, clutching her soft, bulky bag like a teddy bear. Shivers crawled up her spine, and she didn't feel the grin-producing thrill she did when hunting ghosts with Ryan. She'd promised herself that she'd have a great story to tell him when he visited home. He would flip when she regaled him of the dark energy from the corner, the rattle, the cough. Maybe her recorder would catch something she could play for him.

But she needed more proof. She wrested her stiff arms

from the puffy tote bag and set it down beside the chair. She pulled out her birch wood knitting needles, which were bound to a small swatch of scarf she'd started knitting a week ago. Little loop stitches stretched all along the needle in her right hand, and a long length of working yarn untangled from a big, blue, worsted yarn ball inside the bag.

She reminded herself that she wasn't crazy, just ambitious, and started knitting. Knitting could keep her awake on the off chance she got sleepy, though she doubted that would be possible when sitting in a corner where a ghost may have just lurked.

She looped the working yarn twice over the pointer finger of her left hand to create tension. Then she took the sharp tip of the needle in her left hand and slipped it between the two stitches at the top of the needle in her right. She wrapped the yarn around the needle counterclockwise before pulling the stitch through. She then pushed the fresh stitch off the first needle onto the second needle. She continued with the basic knit stitch, transferring stitch after stitch from the first needle to the second, all the while adding a new row of stitches to her scarf.

The light *click-clack-click* of the wooden needles was soothing and meditative. She felt grounded, and she kept the gentle noise in her head as she spoke.

"Is anyone here?" she asked, her voice still hoarse. She

cleared her throat and tried again. "My name is Abby. What's your name?"

She waited. The light, soft static of the EVP scanner followed, but no sounds otherwise. Nothing but silence and the click of her knitting needles.

No answer was not unexpected. Often, spirit boxes would catch sounds or words at frequencies that the human ear could not hear at normal speed. She could listen to the recording tomorrow at slower and faster speeds, so she continued.

"I would like to speak with you, if you don't mind. Is your name Mrs. Witherton?"

Abby's knitting needles filled the silence with their gentle *click–clack–click*.

"Do you know Jacob Myers?"

Click–clack–click.

She reached the end of her row of stitches and flipped the scarf horizontally. She started knitting a new row in the other direction.

"Why do you think you are still here in this house?"

The blue yarn rose from the ball in the canvas bag in a steady stream, flowing into the scarf. Her fingers worked without her conscious thought in a rehearsed rhythm—*in the front, around the needle, pull the stitch through... in, around, pull... in, around, pull...*

"I would like to know more about you," she said. She flipped the scarf over again and started a third row. "Is there anything you wish to tell me?"

Abby's needle slipped. She cursed and winced at the light scratch on the side of her thumb. Half the looped stitches on the needle slid off and unraveled. She narrowed her eyes in the dim lamplight and started again.

"In, around, pull..." she muttered.

Click-clack-click.

Abby stretched out her stiff fingers as she sat at the kitchen table the next morning with an untouched granola bar and a cup of orange juice. The EVP scanner sat in the middle of the table, replaying the recorded static from the night before. Her own voice was asking questions on the recording. She listened hard for an answer, but she couldn't make anything out.

She must have forgotten to ask questions at all after a certain point. She had continued knitting until morning, and only realized she was still doing it when the sun shone in her eyes through a gap in the drapes. She'd shaken herself as if from a trance, wondering where all the hours had gone. But she'd been tired, and knitting was habitual and methodic.

Maybe zoning out wasn't so weird.

Setting aside her confusion, she'd changed into jean shorts and a flowy, white shirt, then grabbed her tote bag and spirit box and carried them down the creaking stairs to the kitchen.

She took a sip of orange juice and fiddled with the recorder to speed it up. She set it back in the center of the table and pulled the blue scarf from her tote bag. The scarf was five feet long by now, and the blue ball of yarn was dwindling. She chose a skein of green yarn and looped the new color over the wooden needle in her right hand. She started knitting the new yarn into the scarf as she listened.

Again, she heard herself asking questions of a prospective ghost, though now, her voice was high-pitched and quick like a chipmunk. Static greeted her questions, though in shorter stretches of time.

She was vaguely aware of a dull throbbing in her hands, and the scratch of a couple of blisters on her fingers, but she ignored the minor pains and kept her ears strained. When she reached the end of her questions, she kept the recording playing, stretching into the long silence when she'd been sitting in the corner, knitting for the rest of the night. She stood up and started circling the table with idle steps as she listened to the static, still knitting with the soothing *click-clack-click* of the needles massaging her ears.

Maybe she would give the scarf to Ryan. He'd complained over the holidays about how cold it was in Maine. Yes, she decided with a smile. He would like a scarf.

The string of thick green yarn caught on a chair leg, but she thought she heard a spike of static on the recording with the quick cadence of a cough, so she didn't bother fixing the snag and kept pacing across the cold linoleum with bare feet, listening hard for another anomaly. Then she leaned over the table and backed up the recording to replay the section with the cough. The static flared, but she didn't hear a cough this time. Was she imagining things?

She frowned and let the recording continue to play. What had truly been hours in the night passed by in less than two at the high-speed setting, but as hard as Abby listened, she couldn't hear any ghostly whispers.

She reached for the EVP scanner again and stumbled on a taut length of yarn. She caught herself on the table, then opened her mouth as she looked around.

The kitchen was filled with countless stretches of green yarn, as if the chairs and table, the huge microwave dials, the mint-green bread box, the chrome cabinet handles, and a cuckoo clock on a wall were fingers extended to create tension, obliging to hold the working yarn aside so that she could keep looping stitches into the scarf. The scarf itself sprawled across the linoleum like a giant python that could wrap three times around a person's neck. Her new skein of yarn was nearly gone.

Maybe she should take a break.

She turned off the recorder and decided she should lie down for a bit. The house was less spooky during the day; it might be easier for her to sleep now than tonight. She hooked the radiation-limiting wallet of the spirit box onto the waistband of her shorts, and then, without thought, she dug into her canvas tote and pulled out the first ball of yarn that came to her fingers. It was violet and a light, sport weight that she'd normally use for socks. She looped it around one needle and knitted the new yarn into the scarf.

She slung her tote bag on her shoulder and picked her way over and under green yarn toward the hallway. The violet yarn fed steadily from the bag as she performed knit stitch after knit stitch. She headed down the hall, leading the lengthening scarf behind her like a piper calling his rats. She started to climb the curved wooden staircase.

The length of violet working yarn looped through a gap under one of the steps before stretching around the railing, creating a pleasant tension in the yarn as she continued knitting.

In, around, pull...
Click-clack-click.
The scarf trailed after her.

A knocking *rat-tat-tat* made Abby sit up so fast that her vision pulsed black for a few seconds. She attempted to steady herself, but something caught her hands in a snare. She tried to pull them apart, but she looked down and saw her fingers all tangled in black yarn that stretched across her palms and from wrist to wrist like a cat's cradle. The thin lines of yarn bit into her skin, and had clearly done so in many other locations because crisscrossed lines were bleeding all over her hands, surrounded by cracked, peeling white skin. Her fingers were red and swollen with raw blisters. Her palms and wrists felt tight and gnarled like she'd been struck by arthritis.

She tugged again with a flare of panic, but she forced herself to breathe and tried to disentangle the threads, one by one. There were no knots, miraculously, and as she wriggled her fingers through tight loops and under little yarn bridges, she saw she was still attached to her knitting needles, which headed the end of a scarf so long, it ran across the floor, over the living room coffee table, around the television set, and all the way along the opposite wall into the kitchen and out of sight.

Another knock rapped into the silence. She looked around for a door; where was the door?

Her eyes widened as goosebumps raised the hairs on the

back of her neck all the way to her scalp.

Yarn was everywhere.

All colors of the rainbow had snagged every piece of furniture and corner in sight, stretching across the room like the cat's cradle that had bound her hands moments ago. She was surrounded by a web from some giant spider, certainly not... she looked at the scarf... certainly not a web of her absent-minded making?

"Abby? Abby, it's Gary Stephens."

She jumped up and tripped over her canvas tote bag on the floor. Balls and skeins of yarn tumbled out, and she frowned when she saw several she didn't recognize. Had she found more yarn somewhere in the house without remembering doing so?

She shoved her knitting needles in her back pocket, with a wince from the fiery sting of her palms, and hurried to the door. The scarf, heavy now from its sheer length, hung off her like a tail.

She hesitated with her swollen hand on the doorknob. She couldn't let Mr. Stephens see the house like this. What would he think of her? What did she think of *herself*? She glanced back at the insane amount of yarn ensnaring the living room. Yarn clung to the antennae of the old-fashioned, boxy television set, wrapped around the stiff yellow couch many times over, strangled the drapes, hooked on picture frames to stretch across opposite walls, and held all four coffee table legs captive.

How did this *happen?*

If Mr. Stephens didn't get an answer, he might look through a window. Worse, he had a key. What if he let himself in?

Her heart pounding, Abby twisted the knob and opened the door the smallest crack.

"Hi, Mr. Stephens," she said. Her voice sounded hoarse and her throat felt scratchy.

Mr. Stephens' bushy eyebrows rose so far, his forehead became one big raisin.

"Abby," he said. "You look, uh... Well, how've you been, sweetheart?"

"Fine," she answered, opening the door a small amount more so she wouldn't seem suspicious. "Everything's fine. The house is great. No complaints."

"That's good to hear. I can see you're enjoying your spring break. Sleepin' in... No need to get all dolled up for school when you don't leave the house." He sent her a wink, but his smile tugged sideways in an uncomfortable-looking way.

"Uh... No, I guess not." Abby glanced down at herself. "Oh, wow. Sorry, I didn't realize I... that you would be coming."

She was wearing the same outfit she'd worn to her room

last she remembered, but the white shirt was wrinkled like crepe paper, and a blotchy, unidentifiable stain smeared the front.

"I should probably take a shower. Nice seeing you, Mr. Stephens." She fluttered her fingers through the cracked door.

Mr. Stephens tried to peer over her head into the house. "You call if you need anything, you hear? I'll be back in a couple of days to get your key and send you on home."

Abby stopped the door with a lurch in her stomach. "A couple of days?"

"Saturday. You losing track of days in there?" He chuckled. "Easy to do while on vacation."

"So, today is..." Her eyes flicked to the side. "Thursday? Today's Thursday?"

"Yes, it is." Mr. Stephens' smile faltered. "You sure you're OK?"

She forced a smile and nodded. "I'm great. See you Saturday."

She shut the door.

Abby pressed her weight against the cool wood that smelled like fresh paint—one of the renovations Jacob Myers was supposed to have finished while staying here. For some reason, he'd abandoned that chore.

Abby felt like there was something she was supposed to

be doing. She'd come to stay here for a reason, but what was it? She pulled her wooden needles out of her back pocket and started knitting, ignoring the burning pain as they rubbed her raw blisters, listening to the *click-clack-click* as she wandered through what felt like a dark maze of her mind.

Click-clack-click.

Her purpose in the house was on the tip of her tongue, at the outskirts of her brain, but as hard as she tried to find it, she could not remember why she was here.

Click-clack-click.

She listened through the door as Mr. Stephens got in his car and drove off. She was house sitting, she knew that much. But there was something else, something to do with... with Ryan? She had something she needed to tell Ryan.

But what?

Click-clack-click.

Abby pushed herself off the door and headed for the kitchen. She stepped over and under stretches of yarn, feeling like a spy in an action movie having to infiltrate high-security laser-traps. She twisted around a corner and ducked under one string while lifting her leg at an awkward angle to step over another. The scarf she was knitting wrapped around her ankle, but she dragged it along as she reached the yellow and gray linoleum floor of the kitchen.

She tried opening a mint-green cabinet above the sink

with both hands, but the yarn threatened to slip off one of her needles. She slid the row of stitches back on before it would all unravel. The wooden needle was slick with fresh blood from her raw hands, but her observation was a mere passing annoyance. She stuck both needles into her disheveled braid behind her head. She opened the cabinet, but it was full of cleaning equipment, not the glasses she was looking for. How had she gone nearly a full week here without knowing her way around the kitchen?

Thursday?

It couldn't be Thursday. She had just gone to the bedroom for a nap on Sunday. That was the last thing she remembered until she'd been startled by Mr. Stephens' knocking, when she'd been sitting on the living room couch.

She opened another cabinet, but a string of yarn was looped from its handle to the cabinet next to it, so it got stuck halfway open. She tried another, then another. Finally, she found one cluttered with glasses. She grabbed one, but jumped back as a glass pill bottle tumbled from the cabinet with a maraca rattle and hit the floor. Somehow, it didn't break; it rolled across the linoleum and hit the bottom of the yellow refrigerator.

Abby's stomach felt queasy. She remembered that sound, but the source drifted away into the blackness of her memory like everything else from the past few days. A sense of dread rumbled in her gut and compelled her to weave her precarious way through the web of yarn to retrieve the pill bottle.

It rattled when she picked it up, sending shivers through her bones, which only made the rattling worse. The glass was clouded, and the label bore faded lettering and peeled at the edges.

She drew a breath of unnatural, icy air as she got the uncanny feeling that someone was standing behind her. She spun around, the pills rattling in their glass cage, but she tripped on a string of yarn that was wrapped around a chair leg. The chair toppled and knocked her onto her back; the pill bottle rattled away from her loose hand. She took wheezy breaths and darted her eyes around, but no one else was in the kitchen.

She shoved the chair over and rolled onto her side. Something hard dug into her hip. She winced, and then frowned when she heard a light static sound. She looked down and saw her EVP scanner hooked onto the waistband of her shorts, just where she'd left it on Sunday afternoon. Her own voice issued from the recording: *"Is anyone here? My name is Abby. What's your name?"*

That's what she'd been doing in the house! She'd been looking for ghosts.

She let out a breath, finally feeling like she had gained solid ground from her flailing psyche. She managed to stand, disentangling herself as best she could from the yarn grasping her every limb. She still gripped the empty glass from the cabinet, so she hobbled to the sink and poured herself some water.

She had no idea how thirsty she was until the cold water touched her tongue. She finished the glass and poured more, gasping for breath before she poured a third. She turned around and leaned back against the sink, taking her time sipping on the third glass. The chill of the glass felt amazing on her throbbing hand, soothing the countless raw blisters.

"I would like to speak with you, if you don't mind. Is your name Mrs. Witherton?" Abby's voice said from the spirit box recording.

She eyed the pill bottle, now resting under a cabinet on the floor. She recalled the dark, supernatural energy that had emanated from the corner of the bedroom during her first night in the house, a presence she had guessed might be the ghost of the widowed hypochondriac, Mrs. Witherton, judging by the distant coughs and rattle of pills she'd heard. But that was before she'd set the EVP scanner to record, and like when she'd listened to the recording before, there was nothing but silence in response to her questions.

"I would like to know more about you. Is there anything you wish to tell me?"

She swore she heard the pill bottle rattle from under the

kitchen cabinet, but it hadn't moved.

Abby set down the glass, feeling the need to do something to distract herself while she fought her chattering mind and quivering body. She reached up to her braid for her knitting needles. She fumbled to get them loose, but they were really stuck. The long, thick scarf dangled from her braid and weighed her head back. She ended up grabbing one needle's sharp point from underneath her braid and tugged it through, along with a long stretch of working yarn that was connected to a ball somewhere in the house, though there was no telling how many objects it had snagged on its way to her head. She grimaced as she pulled at the yarn and her hair at the same time, stinging her scalp.

Finally, she got the needle and working yarn through her braid and down her shoulder. Since the working yarn was now conveniently around the back of her neck, she decided to switch from her favored long-tail knitting style into the Portuguese style, which required the working yarn to loop around the neck to provide tension rather than using her left hand's fingers to hold the yarn taut.

She then wrenched the needle in her left hand down to lower the thick scarf from her scalp to her left shoulder. With the working yarn looped around her neck, she held both needles and the scarf in front of her chest again, where she could comfortably knit her way out of the kitchen.

In, around, pull...
In, around, pull...
Click-clack-click.

A thick strand of her auburn hair looped around her needle. She kept knitting.

Click-clack-click.

Not knowing what else to do, she decided that returning to the bedroom where she'd experienced the potential presence of Samantha Witherton would be a good next step. She had to focus on why she'd come here—anything to wrangle her thoughts from her blacked-out memories and force herself back to reality.

The hallway was another web of yarn, so she ducked and hopped her way through, feeling the pull of her long, wormlike scarf catching on yarn and furniture as it followed. She had to pause to yank it free several times. When she reached the stairs, she stopped to change the setting of the spirit box to live scanning. She then hit the record button, ready to ask new questions, and listen for new answers. Fresh static issued from the scanner's radio frequencies.

She climbed the stairs, crisscrossed with yarn from railing to crooked picture frame corners and nails on the wall, under and over the open gaps between steps, between balusters, and back to the railing. She strained against the ensnaring yarn until she reached the top landing, where she paused when she heard an unmistakable, gargled voice through the static, but she couldn't make out what it said.

She froze, eyes wide, her lips parted, but unable to ask questions like she'd planned. She flipped the scarf over and knitted faster.

In, around, pull...

Click-clack-click.

More low static followed. White gauzy curtains from a small window across the mudroom, at the same level as the top of the stairs, fluttered to the side as if by an indoor breeze. Abby tried to ignore the pain of her fingers' tight joints and her bleeding blisters as she looked through the glass into the back yard, where the scattered, fallen timber of the tool shed splayed like a mangled corpse.

She felt the stark sensation of someone standing behind her again, just like she had in the kitchen.

She looked over her shoulder and saw nothing but a blank wall, but then she shrieked as something small flew from the master bedroom and smashed into the windowpane across the mudroom. She tripped over another piece of yarn so that she hit the upstairs railing, which buckled a little under her weight.

The jack of spades playing card was pinned flat against the window, the leering face staring at her.

Abby knitted faster, her hands blazing pain, but they

seemed to have a mind of their own as she locked eyes with the jack.

Click-clack-click. Click-clack-click.

She felt a pull of the long threads of yarn woven through her braid, connected to the countless stretches of yarn tangled all around the house. She looked down at the newly-knit portion of the scarf; her needles were getting caught in too-tight loops. She growled in frustration and yanked the scarf closer to her chest, but the excess length dangled to the floor, its heavy weight dragging her needles down.

She grabbed the scarf with one hand and pulled a few feet of it through two balusters of the railing before looping some over the back of her neck. The scarf still felt too heavy, so she pulled more through the railing and looped it three times around the bannister and four times around her neck and shoulders to redistribute the weight.

She kept knitting...

In, around, pull...

But her eyes inexorably rose to the jack of spades playing card on the window, and then past it at the fallen tool shed that had caved just like the houses of cards Jacob Myers had built all around the house before his elaborate suicide.

Clickclackclick-clickclackclick...

"Something's wrong," she whispered, the EVP scanner recording her words. That's what Jacob Myers' suicide note had said before his final, "Goodbye."

She had to call Ryan. That was what her mind screamed at her as her knitting needles splintered in her hands. Shards of wood pierced her fingers and punctured the tight stitches of the scarf. She managed to stuff it all in one hand and reached into her back pocket for her phone.

She pulled it out, smearing the screen with blood, but instead of the usual home screen, the thermal imaging app was open. Orange and red splotches outlined the stair railing, the walls, and the small window opposite her.

She felt fresh, powerful shivers, feeling again like someone was standing in the room, watching her. From below.

She held out her phone with a shaking hand and aimed it at the mudroom floor. The mudroom was orange and red, save for one spot. A deep, dark purple shape of a person looked up at her through the thermal imaging camera.

Abby gasped as a sound like a torrential rattle of pills assaulted her ears. She dropped the phone; it smashed into pieces from the twelve-foot drop. She leaned over the railing and screamed as she saw an old woman with wild white hair standing at the foot of the stairs. The woman wore a ragged, 1950s house dress, with a necklace that looked more like a string of white pills than pearls around her gaunt neck. Her face was long and carved with wrinkles. Her eyes were pale and clouded and stared with a hatred so deep, Abby physically felt it drive a hole through her chest.

Abby dropped her splintered, blood-glossed knitting needles and gripped the creaking wooden railing. But she'd knitted her hair *in* the scarf, and it snatched at her braid and tightened *around* her neck so hard that she couldn't breathe. She choked and tried to *pull* the thick yarn from her throat, but the knotted muscles of her tight, blistered hands spasmed.

Her bare foot slipped on the scarf's tail, the yarn slick as ice on the polished wooden floor. Her gut hit the railing with a painful blow, and she tipped... and fell.

So, how do you make a ghost? Abby thought to herself as her vision faded to black.

You knit one.

About the Authors

K.C. Dunford lives in Pueblo, Colorado and is a wife and mother of two. She is the author of *Lost Illumination*, a young adult fantasy novel. Her writing has also appeared in *The Remington Review* and was selected in the *Words and Brushes* worldwide writing competition.

Find her on Facebook and Instagram @KCDunfordBooks.

Peter L. Harmon created High Dive Publishing to help authors take the leap into the daunting waters of publishing. He has always loved spooky stories. He is the author of *The Happenstances…* young adult book series. He lives in the Los Angeles area with his wife, two kids, and their pug, Summer.

Find him on Twitter and Instagram @PeterLHarmon

ANDREW ADAMS is a writer, adventurer, and filmmaker who has produced videos in over thirty countries and six continents. He has climbed mountains and hiked glaciers and kayaked through caves and bungee jumped out of gondolas while shooting, directing, and producing travel content for National Geographic Adventures, Tastemade Travel, and DreamWorksTV. He lives in Los Angeles. He has written and directed narrative film work for Disney XD (*The Fixits*) and CryptTV. He is the creator of two independent comic book series (*Schismatic* and *Revisionaries*).

BECK MEDINA is a young adult author, podcast host, and mindset coach residing in California. She has been publishing under 1537 Press, her independent publishing company, since 2016 and has written two novels, including *A Fantastic Mess of Everything* and *All the Stars on Fire*. Aside from writing, Beck is also a full-time cat mom and pop music lover.

Find her on Twitter and Instagram @BeckMedina

Originally from Seattle, **MALCOLM BADEWITZ** now writes from his kitchen table in Los Angeles. He studied psychology at the University of Washington, where he learned he's a terrible researcher. Now he's writing scripts, most of which deal with horror in one way or another. Pray for him

DANIEL LEE is the author of the novel *After Death*, which won First Place in the Nerdist Sci-Fi Contest and is forthcoming from Inkshares, and his short story "The Grave Ordeal of Jawbone John South" can be found in Writing Bloc's *ESCAPE! An Anthology*. He lives in Los Angeles, where he makes his living as an editor.

See more of his work at Dan-Lee.net.

SEAN CAMERON is from Rochester, England and currently lives in Los Angeles, California. When not laughing at the British weather report, he finds time to write the comedy book series *Rex & Eddie Mysteries*. He likes carrot cake, dinosaurs, and hiking; although not much hiking happens as he fears being eaten by a mountain lion. He dislikes the news, squash soup, and mountain lions.

Find him on Twitter @SeanCameronUK or
Facebook SeanCameronAuthor

BEN GREENE is a writer and actor living in Los Angeles. Most recently, Ben was a writer for the Emmy-nominated animated series, "Hilda" (Netflix), writing multiple episodes for an upcoming season. Ben has previously worked as a staff writer on the DreamWorks animated series "Harvey Girls Forever!" (Netflix) and as a freelance writer on shows like "Talking Tom and Friends " (Netflix) and "The UCB Show" (Starz On-Demand).

Find him on Twitter @BenjaminGreene and
Instagram @BenGreene6

JOE CABELLO is a California-native who has written several *Star Wars* parody books as well as the anime-inspired comic book, *Robot. Black Belt. Champion.* He has worked in TV, film, and games, and aside from writing, he also has worked with

Pre-K to 3rd-grade students for the last decade taking them on ninja adventures for the company Young Ninjas USA.

See more of his work at JoeCabello.com

Matthew Hartwell is a TV and feature writer who lives in Los Angeles, California. There used to be a pond in his backyard, but he drained it as a precaution.

Find him on Twitter @Hartwellish

Around watching the world burn and his rather vanilla day job, *Graham Stone Johnson* is a writer. If it creeps, slithers, manifests, hails from the future, or comes indifferent from light-years away, he's down to tell its story. He shares a small apartment in Los Angeles with his wife, Bethany, who is also a writer, and their 65 lb. lapdog, Penny, who does nothing of import.

Find him on Twitter @Grahamification

CHRISTOPHER MALONE is a Maryland-native who enjoys writing and playing music when he isn't hanging out with his wife and kid. His story, "The Picture", was originally published in *The Dark City Crime and Mystery Magazine*.

KATHERINE FORRISTER is an author of speculative fiction with a love of fantasy, history, science, and romance. Prior to her writing career, she attended Georgia State University, Kennesaw State University, and Gwinnett Technical College, focusing on the subjects of theater and performance studies and veterinary technology. She now lives near Kansas City with her family, where she enjoys local festivals and conventions, hiking, playing open-world video games, and curling up on the sofa to read on cold winter nights.

Find her on Twitter @KatForrister and Instagram @KatherineForrister or on her website KatherineForrister.com

CPSIA information can be obtained
at www.ICGtesting.com
Printed in the USA
FSHW011622230921
84953FS

9 780578 743653